THE RANDOM HOUSE
BOOK OF
FAIRY TALES

THE RANDOM HOUSE BOOK OF

FAIRY TALES

Adapted by Amy Ehrlich
Illustrated by Diane Goode

With an Introduction by Bruno Bettelheim

Random House New York

To my mother, with love. —A.E.

To Peter. —D.G.

Library of Congress Cataloging in Publication Data:
Ehrlich, Amy, 1942–
    The Random House book of fairy tales.
    SUMMARY: Nineteen of the best-known fairy tales, including
"Rapunzel," "Beauty and the Beast," "Thumbelina," and "Hansel and Gretel."
    1. Fairy tales. [1. Fairy tales. 2. Folklore]
I. Goode, Diane, ill.   II. Random House (Firm)   III. Title.
PZ8.E32Ran   1985   398.2′1   83-13833
ISBN: 0-394-85693-7 (trade); 0-394-95693-1 (lib. bdg.)

Manufactured in the United States of America

CONTENTS

INTRODUCTION

We do not know when or how fairy tales were invented. But as a form of literature handed down in the oral tradition, they are as ancient as any literature known to man. They were retold and listened to throughout the ages because they speak about man's fate, his trials and tribulations, his fears and hopes, and his most basic problems: in becoming and proving himself, in relating to his fellow men, and relating to the supernatural. Fairy tales convey to us images of the deeper meaning of life in a pleasing and persuasive form. The widespread preference of today's audiences for films such as Westerns and science fiction sagas such as *Star Wars*—all essentially fairy tales in modern disguise—shows that, as of old, these themes have much to offer to us today and to all ages, but particularly the young.

Freud recognized this when, in his paper on fairy tales, he wrote that "It is hardly surprising to learn through psychoanalysis what great importance fairy tales have for the psyche of our children." These tales are indeed of great help in the development of the psyche of the child. Children, on their own, are often unable to give name, form, or body to either their deepest fears or their most fervent hopes. Without fairy tales, these would remain formless and nameless, the shapeless anxieties which haunt every child in his nightmares, irrespective of whether he experiences them consciously and hence can recall them, or whether they remain repressed and obsess him therefore all the more. These nameless anxieties are much more intractable than well-defined ones, such as those which are described as being experienced by figures in fairy tales.

Taking in these stories permits the child to come to grips with his anxieties as he projects their causes onto evil figures he encounters in the stories, and as he gives body and with it concreteness to his fears in line with events told in the tales. Encountering his anxieties in story form permits the child to familiarize himself with them in an area once removed from his immediate experience, a most important first step toward objectifying and conquering them.

The more definite the source of our anxiety is, the better off we are. It is much better to be afraid of some dangerous animal or witch than of something formless we cannot place or recognize, that hence could be anywhere and everywhere, ready to pounce on us at any moment. Although the child may at moments be fearful of figures such as the witch or wolf or ogre who lives in the sky, if he is at all normal, such fears will not last, since the child is well aware that, being a city dweller or living in a suburb, he is not likely to be abandoned in a deep forest, nor to encounter wolves or beanstalks which grow into the sky on the city streets. Further, the more we can concretize an anxiety, the less ever-present it becomes. If a story giving form to our anxiety takes place in a distant time or place, we can either distance ourselves from it, or sometimes make it our own, as best fits our needs of the moment. So as readers become more familiar with a story and the solution it offers, they are also becoming able to devise methods to pacify their anxiety and thus protect themselves against what causes it.

Fairy tales assure the child that every evil phantom has its opposite which is more powerful in doing good than the evil figure is in doing evil, something the child may not be able to imagine all on his own when overcome by what, at the moment, seem to him the overwhelming difficulties of his life. It is the subtle balance between good and bad powers that is finally tipped in favor of the victory of virtue which gives the child the hope that in real life, his misfortunes will not only be limited in time, but will completely disappear, to be replaced by his elevation to a higher plane of existence where he will be secure for the rest of his life. While in reality there is not always a happy ending to our travails, it is the hope that there might be which sustains us, while without it we may fall into despair.

For the child especially, a collection such as *The Random House Book of Fairy Tales* opens doors to an enchanted universe where, as if through magic, goodness and beauty conquer all. These nineteen classic European fairy tales permit the child to engage in flights of fancy whenever his troubles seem overwhelming, as is all too often the case in his life. No matter how dejected a child may feel at the moment—how unfairly he thinks he is being treated, how clumsy and unlovable he fears to be, how stupid he thinks he is—fairy tales promise him that despite it all, someday he will leave his inferior state far behind and come happily into his own. Then his true merits will be recognized by one and all and his efforts to be good will find their just rewards, while those who pushed him down will meet their deserved punishment. Thus the fairy tale, more effectively than almost any other experience, convinces the child that it is in his best interest to be good and to shun evil. It is the lessons learned from fairy tales and the hopes they nourish which help the child to carry on well and undaunted not only in imagined, but in real adversity. This is the beauty of fairy tales—the way they work their true magic, for all to enjoy.

Bruno Bettelheim
January 1984

THE RANDOM HOUSE
BOOK OF
FAIRY TALES

THE EMPEROR'S NEW CLOTHES

Hans Christian Andersen

In a country far away there was once an emperor who loved nothing better than new clothes. All his money was spent on shirts and doublets and pants and cloaks. He never drove in the woods or went to the theater or reviewed the troops in the army unless it was to show off some new costume. The emperor had clothes for every hour of the day and evening, and whenever his ministers wanted to find him, they had only to look in his dressing room.

Life was very gay in the great town where he lived. The streets were thronged with strangers, and one day two swindlers were among them. They made themselves out to be weavers and said they could weave cloth more beautiful than any on earth. Not only were the colors and patterns superb, but the garments that were made from the cloth had the amazing quality of becoming invisible to all who were dull and incompetent. Or so the swindlers claimed.

"Those must be wonderful clothes," thought the emperor when he heard the story. "By wearing them I shall be able to tell wise men from fools and learn who among my people deserves my trust. Yes, I must have some of that cloth woven for me at once." And he gave the two swindlers large sums of money so they could begin work.

Quickly they set up two looms and pretended to weave,

yet the shuttles were as empty as air. They demanded the finest silk and the purest gold thread, then they packed it away in their bags and worked upon the empty looms far into the night.

After a time the emperor was eager to discover how the weavers were getting on with the cloth. But remembering that anyone who was a fool would not be able to see it, he became reluctant to go into the room himself. "Of course I have no fears about my own competence," he thought. "But still it may be best to send some other man. My oldest minister is the one for the task. He is clever and will be able to judge the quality of the cloth at once."

And so the old minister went to find the weavers. There they sat before their empty looms, working the invisible thread as though it were real. "How can this be?" thought the man, opening his eyes very wide. "I see nothing, nothing at all."

The swindlers stood up then and asked him how he liked the unusual design and the beautiful colors. They pointed to the empty looms and the minister stared as hard as he could, but he could see nothing, for there was nothing. "Could it mean that I am stupid?" he thought fearfully. "I have never thought so, but who can be certain? Nobody must be allowed to know that I cannot see the cloth."

"Well, what do you think of it?" asked one of the weavers.

"Oh, it is beautiful. Most exquisite. I shall certainly tell the emperor how pleased I am," said the minister.

Then the weavers drew him closer to the empty looms. They named the different colors and described the pattern, and the minister listened closely so that he could repeat it all to the emperor.

Now the weavers demanded more money and more silk for their work, but again they put it into their own pockets and went on weaving at the empty looms.

A short time later the emperor sent another minister to learn how the cloth was getting on and if it would soon be ready. The man looked and looked but he could see only the empty looms. He blinked once and then again and still he saw nothing. "I know I am not a fool," he thought. "So it must mean I am unfit for my position. I must never let on that I cannot see the cloth." And he went back to the emperor and praised the beautiful colors and the design he had never seen. Soon everyone in the town was talking about the splendid cloth.

At last the emperor could wait no longer and decided to see

it for himself. Accompanied by a large number of servants and his two faithful ministers, he went into the room where the weavers were working. They moved their hands fast across the looms, yet there was not a strand of silk upon them.

"Is the cloth not magnificent, Your Majesty?" asked the two ministers. "Surely you will agree with all our praise of it." And they pointed to the empty looms, for each thought the others could see the cloth.

The emperor was struck with horror. "What!" he thought. "I see nothing! This is terrible. Am I a fool? Am I unfit to be emperor?" But knowing that the others were awaiting his response, he nodded and smiled and clapped his hands together. "Perfectly wonderful! Superb!" he said, gazing at the empty loom.

"Perfectly wonderful! Superb!" the servants echoed, though they saw no more than the others.

The very next day there was to be a great procession, and everyone agreed that the emperor must lead it dressed in garments sewn from the wonderful cloth. Then the emperor gave each of the weavers a decoration for his buttonhole and the title of Knight of the Loom.

The night before the procession the weavers sat up until dawn, burning sixteen candles so that people would see how hard they were working to get the emperor's new clothes ready. They pretended to take the cloth off the loom. Then they cut it out in the air with a huge pair of shears and stitched it together using needles without any thread. "Now the emperor's new clothes are ready," they announced.

When the emperor went into the room with his ministers and servants, both of the weavers raised one arm in the air as if they were holding something very precious. "These are the pants; this is the coat; here is the mantle," they said. "As you can see, the cloth is as light and delicate as a spider's web. One might almost think one had nothing on, but that is the very beauty of it."

"Yes, oh yes!" everyone cried, staring harder than ever at nothing.

"Please, Your Majesty, you must take off your clothes so we may put the new ones on here before the mirror," the weavers said.

"Of course. Quite so," said the emperor and he took off all his clothes. Then the weavers pretended to fasten something around his waist and tie something else around his neck, and finally they ran their hands along the floor as if they were arranging the train.

Everyone praised the emperor's appearance even though he was wearing nothing. "How well His Majesty looks in the new clothes!" they said. "What a beautiful coat and mantle!"

"The canopy that will be held over Your Majesty is here. The procession is about to begin!" the oldest minister cried.

The emperor turned round and round in front of the mirror as if admiring his reflection. "Very well, I am ready," he announced. He walked with dignity from the weavers' room, and the chamberlains who were to carry the train pretended to lift it from the ground and hold it with their hands in the air.

Then the emperor walked at the head of the procession under the beautiful canopy, and everyone in the streets cried, "Look at the emperor's new clothes. Are they not the most

wonderful he has ever worn?'' They did not dare admit they could see nothing for fear they would be called fools. Never before had the emperor's clothes been so much admired.

"But he has got nothing on," said a little child.

"Oh, listen to the innocent," said the father. And one person whispered to another what the child had said. "He has nothing on. A child says he has nothing on!"

"But he has nothing on!" all the people cried at last.

The emperor felt a shudder go through him, for he knew at once that it was true, but he had to continue to lead the procession. And so he walked on beneath the canopy, and the chamberlains held up the invisible train.

THE SLEEPING BEAUTY IN THE WOOD

Charles Perrault

In a distant land there lived a king and queen who could have no children. Nothing else would give them pleasure, and they moved through their days as if they were in mourning.

But after many, many years the queen at last bore a daughter. The christening was to be magnificent. For the child's godmothers, seven fairies were chosen. Each was to give her a gift, a talent or virtue that would make of the child perfection itself.

After the christening the company returned to the palace, where a great feast had been prepared to honor the seven fairies. Before each one was a golden plate with a knife and fork and spoon set with diamonds and rubies. But just as they were sitting down to eat, a very old fairy came into the hall. She had not been invited because she had shut herself in a high, distant tower for many years and it was thought that she was dead.

The king ordered a place laid for the old fairy, but he could not give her a golden plate with a knife and fork and spoon as the others had, for only seven had been made. The old fairy was outraged and muttered threats beneath her breath. A young fairy who sat nearby heard her. Fearing that the uninvited one might harm the little princess, she hid herself behind the curtains. She wanted to give the last gift of all and in this way perhaps undo any evil that the old fairy was planning.

THE SLEEPING BEAUTY IN THE WOOD

Soon it was time to give the gifts to the princess. The youngest fairy said she would grow up to be beautiful; the next, that she should have the wit of an angel; the third promised her grace; the fourth gave her the gift of dancing; the fifth, the gift of singing; and the last fairy said she would be able to play sweet music on any instrument she took up.

Now it was the old fairy's turn. She came near to the cradle, her head shaking with rage and spite. "The young princess's beauty and accomplishments will not help her," she announced. "For one day she will prick her hand on a tiny spindle and when this happens she will die." The terrible gift made all the company tremble and weep, and the queen could not be comforted.

But at this instant the young fairy who had hidden came from behind the curtains and cried out, "No, my king and queen, your child will not die of this wound. It is true, I have not the power to change an older fairy's gift. The princess will indeed pierce her finger with a spindle. But instead of dying, she shall only fall into a deep sleep. It will last a hundred years, and at the end of it a king's son will come and awaken her."

The young fairy's words were of scant comfort. To avoid the misfortune that had been foretold for his daughter, the king ordered all the spindles in the kingdom to be destroyed; anyone even found spinning was to be put to death.

Fifteen or sixteen years afterward the king and queen were away in the countryside and the young princess was running about in the palace. She went from room to room and came at last into a little garret on top of the tower, where an old woman was spinning with her spindle. The old woman had never heard of the king's orders and so had gone on making her thread in the way of her mother and grandmother before her.

"What are you doing, my good woman?" asked the princess.

"I am spinning, pretty child," said the old woman, for she did not know who the princess was.

"How clever!" said the princess. "How do you do it? Give it to me so I can try."

Either because she was careless or because the old fairy had

ordained it, no sooner had the girl taken the spindle than it pierced her hand and she fell down in a swoon. The good old woman cried out for help. Servants and courtiers and ladies came running from every room in the palace. They threw water upon the princess's face; they unlaced her and struck her on the palms of her hands and rubbed her temples with cologne. But it was no use; nothing would awaken her.

Then the king, who had returned from the countryside, saw that the old fairy's cruel gift had come to pass and his daughter must sleep for a hundred years. By his order she was carried into the finest room in the palace and laid upon a bed embroidered with silver and gold. The color in her face was undimmed and she was as beautiful as ever. It is true that her eyes were shut, but those who listened closely could hear her breathe, so they knew she was not dead.

The young fairy who had saved the princess's life was far away in the kingdom of Matakin, but a dwarf in seven-league boots came there to give her the news. At once the fairy left for the palace in a fiery chariot drawn by dragons. The king greeted her gently and showed her the room where the princess slept. Though the fairy saw that she was well provided for, she thought how sad the princess would be when she woke up alone in that great palace with the people she knew dead and gone.

So she touched everyone with her magic ring. She touched the housekeepers, the maids-in-waiting, the courtiers, the cooks, the scullions, and the footmen. Then she went into the stable and touched the horses and the stable boys. She even touched Puff, the princess's little dog, who was curled up on the bed beside her. At once they all fell fast asleep and would not wake until the princess woke. Everything in the palace was motionless. The spits on the fire with their partridge meats and pheasants stopped turning, and the flames died down and slept.

The king and queen watched the fairy in silence. And when she was done they kissed their beloved daughter good-bye and left the palace forever. Within a quarter of an hour, a great number of trees interlaced with brambles and thorns grew up around the park and formed a hedge so thick that neither man nor beast could penetrate it and so tall that only the tallest turrets of the palace could be seen. In this way the fairy made a magical safe place where the princess could sleep in peace.

★ ★ ★ ★ ★

At the end of a hundred years the son of a king who lived nearby went hunting in the countryside. He asked the people about the turrets he saw in the woods and why the hedge grew there so thickly. Each told him a different story. Some said it was a place full of ghosts; others said the witches went there to hold their sabbath meetings; still others said it was the home of an ogre who caught children and ate them alive.

The prince did not know what to believe. Then a very old man said to him, "Please, Your Highness, more than fifty years past I heard my father say there was at one time in this castle a princess,

17

the most beautiful ever seen. Because she was bewitched she must sleep for a hundred years and could be awakened only by a prince."

Never had the king's son heard of such a marvelous adventure. Fired by love and the desire for glory, he resolved at once to gain entry to the palace. He prepared to cut down the hedge with his sword, but as soon as he came there all the great trees, the bushes, and the brambles parted to let him pass through. He came out upon a broad avenue and at the end of it was the palace. But when he looked behind to see if his servants were still with him, he discovered that the hedge had closed again and he was all alone. However, this did not deter him, for he was a young prince in search of love and glory.

Quickly he walked into the palace courtyard, but what he saw made him stop in amazement. A frightful silence hung over the place and the image of death was everywhere. A score of men were outstretched upon the paving stones, their limbs at grotesque angles. But then the prince saw beside the porters goblets still filled with wine. He leaned down next to them and felt the movement of their chests and then he knew they were alive and had fallen asleep while drinking their wine.

Next he crossed a court paved with marble and came into a guard room. Guards were standing in their ranks with their muskets on their shoulders and snoring with all their might. He went upstairs and through several rooms filled with people, men and women both. Some were standing and others were sitting, but all were sleeping soundly.

Finally he entered a gilded chamber where he saw upon a bed embroidered with gold and silver a girl of fifteen or sixteen years. Her coral lips were parted slightly and her beauty was so luminous that she seemed almost to shine. The prince approached her, trembling, and fell upon his knees.

THE SLEEPING BEAUTY IN THE WOOD

Then, as the end of the enchantment had come, the princess awoke. She gazed at the king's son tenderly as if she already knew him. "Is it you, my prince?" she said at last. "You have waited a long time."

The prince was thrilled by her words and told her that he loved her better than he did himself. They spoke for many hours, and though their conversation made little sense, it hardly mattered. The princess laughed merrily and nodded at the prince's remarks. It was almost as if she had imagined the moment of her awakening many times over and knew what he would say. Perhaps the good fairy, during so long a sleep, had given her very pleasant dreams.

In the meantime all the palace had woken with the princess. They were naturally concerned with their own needs, and since they were not in love, they were ready to keel over with hunger. The lady of honor at last lost patience and told the princess that dinner must be served. At this the prince helped her up from the bed. Her clothing was magnificent, but he took care not to tell her that she was dressed like his grandmother.

They went together into the great mirrored hall, where they ate their meal to the old-fashioned melodies of violins and oboes that had been silent for a hundred years. After supper the chaplain married them in the palace chapel without losing any time. That night they slept little, as the princess was so well rested and they still had much to say. And in the morning, as dawn was breaking, they traveled to the prince's city where his parents eagerly awaited them.

THE ELVES AND THE SHOEMAKER

The Brothers Grimm

There was once a shoemaker who became poorer and poorer as the years went by. At last he had leather enough only for one pair of shoes. In the evening he cut out the pattern and then he went to sleep.

The next morning he took up a needle and thread, meaning to sew the shoes. But there they stood, neatly sewn and finished on his table. The shoemaker could not believe his eyes. Not a stitch was out of place and the work was better than any he had ever seen.

As he held the shoes, marveling at them, a customer entered the shop. He was so pleased with the shoes that he paid far more than the ordinary price, and the shoemaker was able to buy leather for two pairs more.

He cut them out in the evening, and the next morning prepared to begin work. But there was no need for it because the shoes had already been made and were as well stitched and handsome as the other pair. The first two customers who came into his shop bought them for a good price. And this time the shoemaker was able to buy leather enough for four pairs.

Early the next morning the four pairs of shoes were finished as before. And so it went. What the shoemaker cut out at night was finished in the morning, and customers were never lacking. Soon the shoemaker became a wealthy man.

Always he wondered about the skill of the work, and one

evening not long before Christmas he said to his wife, "How would it be if we were to sit up tonight to see who has been helping us these many months?"

She agreed at once and so they did not go to bed, but lit a candle and hid themselves in a corner of the room. Just at midnight two tiny little men came and sat down at the shoemaker's table. They wore no clothes and said not a single word, but immediately began to work. They stitched and hammered and sewed so neatly and quickly that the shoemaker was amazed. As soon as everything was finished and stood upon the table, they ran quickly away.

"The little men have made us rich and I think we ought to thank them," said the shoemaker's wife in the morning. "They ran about with nothing on and must freeze with cold. Now I shall sew them tiny shirts and pants and coats and knit them caps and socks. And you must make them each a pair of shoes."

The shoemaker and his wife worked hard all day and had everything ready by evening. Then they hid themselves to see how the little men would receive their presents.

At midnight the two came back into the room and sat down at the table. But instead of the leather cut out and waiting, they found the wonderful little clothes.

First the little men were surprised and then they were delighted. They put on the shirts and pants, the coats and socks and caps, and they buckled the tiny shoes upon their feet. When they were done they ran their hands up and down the pretty clothes and admired each other, singing:

> "Now that we're boys so fine and neat,
> Why cobble more for others' feet?"

They hopped and danced about the shoemaker's shop, leaping over chairs and tables and then out the door. From this night on the two little men came back no more, but the shoemaker continued to do well as long as he lived and had good luck in all he attempted.

RAPUNZEL

The Brothers Grimm

A man and his wife had long wished for a child, and after many years had passed it seemed that at last they were to have one. Their house was in the countryside and at the back was a little window that overlooked a beautiful garden planted with vegetables and flowers. But it was surrounded by a high wall and no one dared go in there, for it belonged to a powerful witch.

One day the wife was standing by the window and looking down into the garden when she saw a bed of rapunzel greens. They looked so fresh and lovely that she longed for some to eat. Each day her longing increased until she became pale and sickly and would take no other food. Then her husband was alarmed and said, "What is the matter, dear wife?"

"Ah," she answered, "if I cannot have some of the rapunzel from the garden behind our house, I shall surely die."

Her husband, who loved her, knew he would have to bring her the rapunzel she wanted, no matter what the cost. At twilight he climbed over the wall into the witch's garden. Quickly he picked a handful of the rapunzel and took it to his wife. She made a salad and ate it greedily, but she was still not satisfied. The taste was so wonderful that she had to have more of the rapunzel at once. She wept and begged until her husband agreed to go back into the witch's garden.

Again in the twilight he set out, but this time when he climbed over the wall he saw the witch standing before him.

"How dare you come into my garden and steal my rapunzel?" she said angrily. "You will have to suffer for it."

The man was terribly afraid. "Please take pity on me," he answered. "I had to come here. My wife saw the rapunzel from the window and her longing for it is so great that she will die if she cannot have some."

Then the rage left the witch's face and she said, "If what you say is true, I shall allow you to take away as much as you want—but on one condition. You must give me the child your wife is carrying. I will bring it up as my own and care for it like a mother."

In his fear the man consented to everything, and when the baby was born the witch came for her and gave her the name Rapunzel.

As the years went by, Rapunzel grew to be the most beautiful child imaginable. When she was twelve, the witch took her away and shut her up in a tower that stood in a forest. It had neither staircase nor doors and only a little window high up in the wall. Each time the witch wanted to come in, she would stand below it and cry:

"Rapunzel, Rapunzel,
Let down your hair."

Rapunzel had magnificent long hair, as fine as spun gold. When she heard the witch's voice, she would unfasten her braids and twist them round a hook by the window. Then the hair would fall twenty feet down and the witch would climb up on it.

Some time later it happened that the king's son was riding through the forest and passed close by the tower. As he did he heard a song so lovely and clear that he stood still to listen. Rapunzel sang each day in her loneliness and it was her voice that he heard. The king's son wanted to climb up to her and looked for a door to the tower, but none was to be found.

He rode home but his thoughts were haunted by Rapunzel's sweet song, and he returned again and again to the forest to listen to it. Once, when he was hidden behind a tree, he saw a witch come to the tower and call out:

"Rapunzel, Rapunzel,
Let down your hair."

Then Rapunzel lowered her hair and the witch climbed up to her. "If that is the ladder one must climb, I too shall try it," he said to himself. And the next day, when it began to grow dark, he went to the tower and cried:

"Rapunzel, Rapunzel,
Let down your hair."

At once the hair was lowered and the king's son climbed up on it.

Rapunzel was terrified, for she had never seen a man, but the king's son spoke to her gently and told her how beautiful her song had been. Then she lost her fear, and when he asked if she would have him for her husband, she agreed. She could see that he was young and handsome and she thought that he was kind. "He will love me better than old Mother Gothel does," she said to herself, and she laid her hand in his.

"I will gladly go with you," she told him. "But I do not know how I am to get down from this tower. I'll tell you what. When you come each evening, you must bring me a skein of silk to twist into a ladder. As soon as it is long enough I will come down upon it and we will ride away on your horse."

The witch knew nothing until one day Rapunzel said to her, "Tell me, Mother Gothel, why is it you are so much heavier to draw up than the young prince?"

"Oh, you wicked child!" cried the witch. "I thought I had

separated you from all the world and yet you have deceived me." In her rage she seized Rapunzel's beautiful hair, twisted it twice round her left hand, and cut it off with a pair of shears. When the hair lay upon the ground, she took poor Rapunzel into a vast wilderness and abandoned her there.

In the evening the witch returned to the tower and fastened the hair onto a hook by the window. She waited until the prince came and called:

"Rapunzel, Rapunzel,
Let down your hair."

And then she lowered it. The prince climbed up, and there, crouched beneath the window, was the witch, who glared at him with rage and wickedness.

"Ah," she cried mockingly, "you have come to fetch your love. But the pretty bird has flown from her nest and she can sing no more. Rapunzel is lost to you. Never shall you see her again."

In his pain and grief the prince leaped from the tower, and though he was not killed, his eyes were pierced by the thorns among which he fell. Weeping and lamenting, he roamed about blindly in the forest and had nothing but roots and berries to eat. After many years of wandering alone he at last came into the wilderness where Rapunzel lived in poverty and wretchedness.

The prince heard a clear, sweet voice and it seemed so familiar to him that he went toward it. Rapunzel knew him at once and fell weeping upon his neck. Two of her tears wetted his eyes and they grew clear again so he could see all that was before him.

Then he took Rapunzel back to his kingdom, where they were greeted with great rejoicing, and they lived for a long time afterward in happiness and peace.

THE TWELVE DANCING PRINCESSES

The Brothers Grimm

Once there was a king who had twelve daughters and each was more beautiful than the next. They slept side by side in a great hall that he locked and bolted each night. But every morning, when the king unlocked the door, he saw that the shoes by the sides of their beds had been worn out from dancing. The princesses would not say where they had been and no one could explain the mystery. At last the king sent out a proclamation that any man who discovered where the princesses danced could choose one of them for his wife and someday become king. But whoever came forward and failed to learn the answer after three days and three nights was to be put to death.

A prince soon presented himself and agreed to take up the challenge. He was brought into a small room next to the hall where the princesses slept. His bed was made up there and he was to watch them all through the night. Though the prince tried to stay awake, his eyes grew heavy and he could not. In the morning the princesses' shoes had again been worn out from dancing and the young man had no answer for it. The second and third nights were the same, and on the morning of the last, the young man's head was cut off without mercy. Many others came after him but they too lost their lives.

Now it happened that a poor soldier found himself on the king's road. There he fell in with an old woman who asked him where he was bound.

"I hardly know myself," he answered, and added in jest, "Perhaps I should discover where the king's daughters dance each night so I can wed one and become king."

"That is not so difficult," said the old woman. "Only listen closely. You must not drink the wine that will be brought to you in the evening, but must pretend to be asleep." Then she gave him a short cloak, saying, "When you wear this you will be invisible and then you can slip out after the twelve princesses."

The soldier thanked the old woman for her kindness and went before the king. He was as well received as the others. Servants dressed him in royal garments and led him into the small room.

All was as the old woman had said. When evening came and he was preparing to go to bed, the eldest princess appeared, bringing him a cup of wine. But the soldier had tied a sponge under his chin and he let the wine run into it without drinking a single drop. He lay down and was quiet for a time and then he pretended to snore.

The twelve princesses heard him and began to laugh. "So he too must lose his life," the eldest said.

With no attempt at secrecy they sprang from their beds, opened cupboards and chests, and brought out their most beautiful dresses. They fastened their shoes and combed their hair, admiring themselves before the glass. Only the youngest princess held back. "You may rejoice," she said, "but I feel very strange. Some misfortune is certainly going to befall us tonight."

"You silly goose!" answered the eldest. "Have you forgotten how many men have lost their lives? I don't know why I even bothered to give this one a sleeping potion. The fool would never have awakened anyway."

When they were all ready, they tiptoed into the room for a last look at the soldier, but his eyes were closed and he did not stir. Then the eldest went to her bed and knocked on it. At once it sank into the earth and the twelve princesses descended into the opening, one after another, with the eldest leading the way.

Without a moment's hesitation the soldier threw on his invisible cloak and went after them, following behind the youngest. Halfway along the passageway his foot caught the hem of her dress. She was frightened and cried out, "What was that? Who is holding on to my dress?"

"Don't be so foolish. You must have snagged it on a hook," said the eldest. They kept on going, and when they were quite underground they stood on a beautiful broad avenue lined with

trees. Though it was a dark night the leaves on the trees were silver and they glittered and shone.

"I must take some away with me," the soldier thought. He broke off a twig and a great crash came from the tree.

The youngest cried out again. "Something is the matter, I tell you. Did you not hear that sound?"

"It is the fanfare of trumpets because we shall soon release our princes from their enchantment," the eldest said.

Next they came to an avenue where all the leaves on the trees were of gold, and at last into a third where the leaves were shining diamonds. The soldier broke off a twig from each and it made such a crack each time that the youngest princess was afraid, but the eldest still said it was the fanfare of trumpets.

They went on until they came to a great lake. By the shore were twelve little boats and in each sat a handsome prince. The princes had been waiting for the twelve princesses and each took

one with him, but the soldier seated himself by the youngest.

"I don't know why the boat is so much heavier tonight," said her prince. "I must row with all my strength to move it."

"Perhaps it is the weather. It is strangely hot and still outside," the princess said, but she was not really certain.

Across the lake stood a splendid castle with lights glowing in every window. Drums and trumpets played music for a ball. They rowed across and each prince danced with the one he

loved, and the soldier danced too, silently and unseen. If one of the princesses held a cup of wine he drank from it so that it was empty when she brought it to her mouth. The youngest was alarmed by this, but the eldest always silenced her in a mocking way. They danced until three o'clock in the morning, when their shoes were danced into holes and they were forced to stop. Then the princes rowed them back again across the lake, but this time the soldier sat with the eldest. On the opposite shore they said good-bye to their princes and promised to return the following night.

When they came to the stairs leading back to their chamber, the soldier ran ahead of them. By the time they came into his room he was lying in bed, snoring loudly. "Well, we are quite safe from this one," the eldest princess said. Then they took off their beautiful dresses, placed their worn-out shoes by the sides of their beds, and lay down to sleep.

The next morning the soldier resolved not to speak of it so he could see such marvelous things again. He went with the princesses the second and third nights and all was the same as the first time. They danced until their shoes were full of holes, and on the last night the soldier took a wine cup away from the ball.

When the time came for him to give his answer, he took the three twigs and the cup with him and went before the king. The twelve princesses stood behind the door, listening to hear what he would say.

"Where do my daughters go when they dance their shoes to pieces each night?" asked the king.

"It is in an underground place where there are twelve princes waiting," said the soldier. Then he told the king of all he had seen, and when the story was done he brought out the objects he had taken.

At once the king summoned his daughters and asked them
if the soldier had spoken the truth. As they saw that they had
been betrayed and would gain nothing by lies, they were forced
to confess everything. Then the king asked the soldier which one
of them he would choose for a wife. "I am no longer young,"
the soldier answered, "so I shall take the eldest."

The wedding was celebrated that very day and the kingdom
was promised to him after the king's death.

JACK AND THE BEANSTALK

Old English

There was once a widow who had a son named Jack and a cow called Milky White. They were very poor and had only the milk from the cow, which they sometimes sold for food. But one morning Milky White gave no milk at all and they didn't know what to do.

"Do not worry, Mother," said Jack at last. "Today is market day. I shall take Milky White with me and sell her. She is a fine-looking cow and will fetch enough money to start us up in a trade."

So he took the cow's halter in his hand and set off for town. He hadn't gone far when he met a funny-looking old man along the road. "Good morning, Jack," he said.

"Good morning to you," said Jack, wondering how the man knew his name.

"Well, Jack, and where are you off to?"

"I'm going to market to sell our cow here."

"You seem the sort of lad who will get a good price," said the man. "I wonder if you know how many beans make five."

"Two in each hand and one in your mouth," said Jack, quick as a wink.

"Right you are," said the man. "And here they are, the very beans themselves." He took from his pocket a number of beans, unlike any Jack had ever seen before. "These are magical beans,

Jack. Plant them at night and by morning they'll grow right up to the sky."

"You don't say!" said Jack.

"I do indeed," the stranger told him. "And since you are such a clever lad, I'll happily swap them for your cow there."

"It's a deal," said Jack. And he handed over Milky White and pocketed the beans.

Back home Jack went. It wasn't even dusk when he came through the door.

"Home already?" his mother said. "I see you haven't got Milky White so you must have sold her. How much did she fetch? Five pounds?"

Jack smiled and shook his head.

"Ten?"

Jack shook his head again.

"Can it have been twenty pounds?" said his mother, clapping her hands with excitement.

"No, Mother," said Jack. "I got something better still." He opened his hand to show the beans. "Plant them at night and in the morning—"

"You dolt! You idiot!" his mother screamed. "You gave away my Milky White, the best milker in the district and prime beef besides, for a handful of beans? I'll teach you!" Then she threw the beans out the window, thrashed Jack soundly, and sent him to bed without his supper.

In the morning when Jack woke up, the room looked very strange. Shadows of leaves were on the walls and the sun did not shine through the window. Quickly he got dressed and went to look outside. There right next to the house grew a huge beanstalk that went up and up and up until it reached the sky. Jack couldn't see the top of it and then he knew that the man had spoken the truth.

He threw open his window and climbed right onto the beanstalk. It grew straight and true, just like a ladder leading up to the sky. Higher and higher Jack climbed until he came out upon a long, broad road. So he walked along and walked along until he came to a great big tall house. On the doorstep there was a great big tall woman.

"Good morning, to you, ma'am," said Jack politely. "Could you kindly give me some breakfast? I've had nothing to eat from midday past and it was a long walk to get here."

"It's breakfast you want, is it?" said the great big tall woman. "It's breakfast you'll be if you don't move off from here. My man is an ogre and there's nothing he likes better than boys broiled on toast. You'd best be moving on, for he'll soon be coming."

"Oh, please, ma'am, give me something to eat," said Jack. "My stomach is so empty. I may as well be broiled as die of hunger."

Well, the ogre's wife was not a stingy woman, so she took Jack into her kitchen and gave him bread and cheese and a jug of milk. Jack wasn't half finished with it when—*thump! thump! thump!*—the house began to shake.

"Hurry, hurry!" the ogre's wife said. "It's my man. He's coming. You can jump in here." And she pushed Jack into the oven just as the ogre walked through the door.

He was a big one, to be sure. At his belt he had three calfs strung up by the heels, and he unhooked them and threw them on the table. "Here, wife, broil me a couple of these for breakfast. Ah! What's this I smell?" He looked all around him and said:

"Fee fi fo fum,
I smell the blood of an Englishman.
If he's alive or if he's dead,
I'll use his bones to grind my bread."

"Nonsense, dear, you must be dreaming," said his wife. "Here, go and wash up and by the time you come back, your breakfast will be ready."

Jack was just about to jump out of the oven and run away when the woman told him not to. "Wait until he has his nap," she said.

With a great deal of munching and licking of lips, the ogre ate the calfs. Then he went to a big chest and took from it two

bags of gold. Down he sat and counted the gold until his head began to nod and his snores shook the house.

Jack crept out of the oven and grabbed one of the bags of gold. Off he ran as fast as his legs would carry him. When he reached the beanstalk, he threw the bag of gold into his mother's garden and climbed down himself. Down and down and down he climbed until he was home. "See, Mother," he said, handing her the bag of gold. "The beans were magic and that's all there is to it."

Jack and his mother lived on the bag of gold for some time, but at last they came to the end of it. With hunger gnawing at his belly, Jack made up his mind to try his luck at the top of the beanstalk again.

On a fine morning he woke up early and got onto the beanstalk from his window. He climbed and he climbed and he climbed until he came out on the road again. Then he walked along and walked along until he saw the great big tall woman standing on her doorstep.

"Good morning, ma'am," said Jack, bold as you please. "Could you be so kind as to give me something to eat?"

"Go away, my boy," the big tall woman said, "or else my man will have you for breakfast." Then she drew back and looked Jack in the eye. "But aren't you the same lad who came here once before? Do you know, that very day my man missed one of his bags of gold."

"That's strange, ma'am," said Jack. "I daresay I could tell you something about it, but I'm so hungry I can't speak."

Well, the big tall woman was so curious that she took him into her kitchen and gave him some food. Scarcely had Jack begun to eat when—*thump! thump! thump!*—they heard the giant's footsteps.

"Quick! Into the oven with you!" said his wife.

In came the giant, sniffing the air and looking all around him. "Fee fi fo fum, I smell the blood of an Englishman," he said as he had the first time. His wife did not let on that Jack was there, but broiled three oxen for his breakfast.

Then the giant said, "Wife, bring me the hen that lays the golden eggs." When she did so, the ogre said, "Lay!" and the hen laid an egg of solid gold. Now it was time for his nap. Soon his head began to nod and his snores shook the house.

Jack crept out of the oven, caught hold of the golden hen,

and was off as fast as his legs could carry him. But this time the hen gave a cackle that woke the ogre. "Wife," he yelled, "what have you done with my hen?"

"Why do you ask, my dear?" she answered.

But that was all Jack heard, for he ran off to the beanstalk and climbed down faster than the first time. When he got home he showed his mother the wonderful hen. "Just another creature to feed," she said.

Then Jack said to the hen, "Lay!" and it laid an egg of solid gold.

Each day Jack told the hen to lay another egg and though she always did so, he still longed for adventure. At last he decided to climb the beanstalk once more. But this time Jack knew better than to go straight to the great big tall house, as the ogre's wife would surely betray him. Instead he waited behind a bush until he saw her come out with a pail of water. Then he dashed into the house and hid himself in the coal scuttle. He had been there for only a short time when he heard *thump! thump! thump!* and the ogre came in with his wife.

"Fee fi fo fum, I smell the blood of an Englishman!" cried the giant in a rage. "I smell him, wife! I smell him!"

"Do you, my dear?" she answered. "If it's that same lad who stole your bag of gold and the hen that laid the golden egg, he's sure to be in the oven." They both rushed there at once, but of course Jack wasn't there.

So the ogre sat down to breakfast, but every now and then he muttered, "Well, I could have sworn . . ." and he got up and searched the larder and the cupboards and looked behind the door. But he never thought of the coal scuttle.

After he had eaten, the ogre called out, "Wife, wife, bring me my golden harp." So she brought it and set it on the table before him. Then the ogre said, "Sing!" and the harp sang and went on singing until the ogre fell asleep.

As soon as the ogre's snores began to shake the house, Jack lifted the lid of the coal scuttle and crept on his hands and knees over to the table. Quickly he took the golden harp, then dashed toward the door. But the harp called out loudly, "Master! Master!" and the ogre woke in time to see Jack running off with his harp.

Jack ran as fast as he could and the ogre came rushing after. Closer and closer he came until Jack could feel his hot breath burning him. But Jack ran down the long broad road and swung himself onto the beanstalk. The giant hesitated, for he did not like to trust himself to such a spindly plant. But the harp called again, "Master! Master!" and the ogre followed Jack down.

The beanstalk trembled and swayed beneath the ogre's weight. Jack was sorely frightened, but he was almost home now and could see his mother standing in the garden. "Mother! Mother!" he called out. "Bring an axe! Bring an axe!"

She came rushing up with the axe in her hands. Then she saw the ogre's legs just coming through the clouds and stood stock-still with terror.

But Jack jumped down and got hold of the axe and swung it at the beanstalk with all his might. With two chops the beanstalk was cut in two. The giant held on for dear life, but it was no use; he was dead as soon as he hit the ground. Then Jack and his mother buried the giant and the beanstalk with him.

They became very rich from selling the golden eggs and making the golden harp play for the curious. Jack's mother's scolding tongue was still and all their days were happy.

SNOW WHITE

The Brothers Grimm

Long ago in wintertime a queen sat by a window sewing. The snowflakes swirled down through the sky past the frame of the window, which was made of black ebony. Suddenly the queen pricked her finger with the needle and three drops of blood fell upon the snow. The colors were so strong and beautiful that she thought at once: "If only I could have a child as white as snow, as red as blood, and as black as ebony."

Soon afterward the queen gave birth to a daughter who was white as snow, red as blood, and had hair as black as ebony. She was called Snow White, and when she was born, the queen died.

After a year had passed the king took another wife. She was very beautiful but so proud that she could not bear to think that anyone might surpass her. She had a magical looking glass and day after day she stood before it and admired herself, saying:

"Looking glass, looking glass, on the wall,
Who in the land is fairest of all?"

And the glass answered:

"Thou, O Queen, are fairest in the land."

Then the queen was happy, for she knew that the looking glass spoke the truth.

But Snow White was growing up and each day she became more beautiful. And when she was seven years old, she was as beautiful as the morning and far more beautiful than the queen. Then when the woman stood before her looking glass and said:

"Looking glass, looking glass, on the wall,
Who in the land is fairest of all?"

it answered:

"Thou, Queen, may fair and lovely be,
But Snow White is fairer still than thee."

The queen was horrified. She whirled around and left the room and her heart was filled with envy. From that day, whenever she looked at Snow White, the queen hated her. At last she could neither eat nor sleep, so consumed was she with hatred for the girl. Then she called to her side a huntsman and said to him, "Take the child into the darkest part of the forest. I can no longer bear the sight of her. Kill her and bring me back her lung and liver so I will know that she is dead."

The huntsman obeyed and took Snow White away. But

when he had drawn his knife and was about to pierce her heart, she began to weep. "Please, huntsman, spare my life. I will run away into the forest and never return again."

And she was so innocent and beautiful that the huntsman took pity upon her. "Run away, then, child. I will not hurt you," he said. He thought the wild animals would soon kill her, and yet he felt as if a stone had been rolled from his heart because he would not be the one to do it. Just then a young boar came running by, so he stabbed it and cut out its lung and liver and took them to the queen. The cook had to prepare them for supper, and the queen ate them, certain now that Snow White had been killed.

But now the child was all alone in the forest, with the great dark trees arching above her. She was terrified and began to run. She ran over rocks and through brambles, and the wild animals saw her but did her no harm.

She ran as long as she could and as far as she could, and at evening she saw in the distance a little cottage with sparkling windows and a red tiled roof. She was tired and so she went there to rest. Inside everything was small, but neat and clean and pretty. A table with a white cloth had been laid for supper, and Snow White saw seven plates and seven spoons and seven cups. Against the wall stood seven little beds side by side.

She was so hungry and thirsty that she ate some vegetables and bread from each plate and drank a drop of wine from each cup. Then, as she was weary, she lay down upon each bed to find a comfortable one, and the seventh bed was just right. She pulled up the white coverlet and soon fell fast asleep.

When it was dark the owners of the cottage returned. They were seven dwarfs who mined for copper and gold deep in the mountains. They lit their seven candles and saw that someone had eaten their food and drunk their wine and lain upon their

beds. And when the seventh dwarf came to his bed, he saw Snow White sleeping there. He called to the others, and they gathered around and held up their candles so that the light fell upon her face. "Oh, what a lovely child!" they said. Then they did not wake her but let her sleep undisturbed. The seventh dwarf stayed with the others, one hour in each bed, until the night was gone.

At dawn Snow White awoke. She was frightened when she saw the seven dwarfs, but they treated her gently and asked her her name and how she had come to be there. "My name is Snow White," she said and she told them everything.

The dwarfs felt very sorry for the girl who had come so near to death, and they agreed that she should stay in the cottage. "If you will take care of our house and have our suppers ready at night, you shall want for nothing," they told her. Snow White was happy then and said she would do all that they asked.

Each morning they went off to their work in the mountains and each evening when they came home, the supper was hot and the house was sparkling. But the dwarfs warned Snow White that she would be alone all day and must let no one in. "Beware of your stepmother," they said. "She will soon know you are here and then she will come after you."

Although the queen believed Snow White was dead, it was not long before she went again to her looking glass and said:

> "Looking glass, looking glass, on the wall,
> Who in this land is fairest of all?"

And the looking glass answered:

> "Over the hills where the seven dwarfs dwell
> Snow White is there, alive and well,
> And none is so fair as she."

Then the queen knew that the huntsman had betrayed her and Snow White was still alive.

Her envy sprang up again, stronger than the first time, and so she determined to kill the girl herself. She thought and thought about how to do it, and then she painted her face and dressed herself as a pedlar woman. No one would have known her as she set off through the woods, hobbling on a stick. When at last she came to the dwarfs' house, she knocked upon the door. "Pretty wares to sell! Pretty wares to sell!" she cried.

Snow White looked out the window and saw that it was only an old pedlar woman who was holding up a bundle of apron ties woven in bright silks. "Surely I can let her in," thought the girl, and she unbolted the door and bought the pretty ties.

"Don't you see, child, you must lace yourself more tightly," said the old woman. Snow White suspected nothing, but stood before her and let herself be laced with the new ties. But the old

woman laced her so tightly that she lost her breath and fell down as if she were dead.

Not long afterward the seven dwarfs returned. They were frightened when they found Snow White pale and motionless upon the floor. But as soon as they lifted her up they saw that she was laced too tightly and they cut the ties with a knife. Then the girl began to breathe again and soon recovered.

When she told them what had happened, they said, "But the old pedlar woman was the wicked queen, who would do anything to be rid of you. Be sure to take care and let no one in."

As soon as the queen reached home she went to her glass and said:

"Looking glass, looking glass, on the wall,
Who in this land is fairest of all?"

And it answered as before:

"Over the hills where the seven dwarfs dwell
Snow White is there, alive and well,
And none is so fair as she."

When she heard this the queen was struck with fear, for she knew that Snow White had not been killed. The queen had some knowledge of witchcraft and decided to make a poison comb. She hid it with several others and then disguised herself, taking the shape of a different old woman. She set off across the seven hills to the house of the seven dwarfs and knocked upon the door. "Good things to sell! Good things to sell!" she cried.

Snow White looked out the window and said, "Go away, please. I dare not let anyone in."

"But you must only look," said the old woman and she held out the poison comb for Snow White to see.

It was such a pretty comb, so delicate and fine, that the girl let herself be persuaded to open the door.

"Now, child, I shall comb your hair properly," said the old woman and she ran the comb through Snow White's ebony hair. At once the poison took effect and Snow White swooned to the floor. "That will be an end to you," said the woman and she went away.

But it was nearly evening and soon the dwarfs came home.

When they saw Snow White lying as if she were dead, they suspected the queen and searched until they found the poisoned comb. Scarcely had they taken it from her head when Snow White awoke and told them what had happened. Then they warned her once again to take care and to open the door to no one.

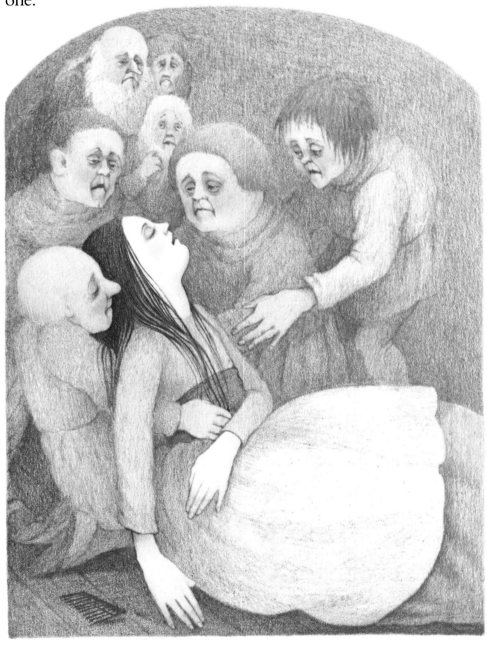

The queen, at home, went to her looking glass and said:

"Looking glass, looking glass, on the wall,
Who in this land is fairest of all?"

Then it answered again:

"Over the hills where the seven dwarfs dwell
Snow White is there, alive and well,
And none is so fair as she."

When the queen heard the glass say this, she trembled and shook with rage. "Snow White must die," she cried, "even if it costs me my life!" She went into a secret room high at the top of the palace where no one ever came, and there she made a poisonous apple. The shape was perfect and the outside shone red and white. It was so tempting that anyone who saw it must long for it, but whoever ate a piece would surely die.

The queen dressed herself as a peasant's wife and painted her face. Then she went over the seven hills to the seven dwarfs' house and knocked upon the door.

At once Snow White looked out the window and said, "I dare not let anyone in. The seven dwarfs have told me not to."

"I shall stay outside then," said the peasant woman. "Only taste one of my apples. They are so fresh and sweet."

"No, I dare not take it," said Snow White.

"What? Are you afraid of poison, you silly child? See, I will cut the apple in two. You shall have the red part and I will take the white." The apple was so cleverly made that only the red part was poisoned, but when Snow White saw that the peasant woman was unharmed, she could resist no longer and she held out her hand for the fruit.

The moment she bit into it, she fell dead upon the ground. The apple's poison had done its work. "White as snow, red as

blood, black as ebony!" the queen cried. "This time nothing can save you!"

When she went home she said to her looking glass:

"Looking glass, looking glass, on the wall,
Who in the land is fairest of all?"

it answered:

"Thou, O Queen, are fairest in the land."

And at last her envious heart was glad.

In the evening the dwarfs found Snow White lying on the ground. She did not breathe or move, and though they undid her apron ties and washed her face with wine and water, it was no use; the child was dead. So they laid her upon a bier and all seven watched and mourned her for three days' time.

They were going to bury her, but her black hair shone and

her cheeks were red and pretty as if she were still alive. "We cannot hide her in the dark ground," they said, so they had a coffin made for her of transparent glass. They laid Snow White in it and in golden letters they wrote her name and that she was the daughter of a king. Then they put the coffin out upon the hill and took turns watching it, one at a time. And the birds came too and mourned Snow White; first an owl, then a raven, and at last a dove.

Snow White lay for a long, long time in the coffin and she did not change, but looked as if she were only sleeping, for she was even now white as snow, red as blood, and black as ebony.

Then it happened that a king's son came into the forest and saw the coffin upon the hill. He knelt down before the beautiful Snow White and read the golden letters. Then he went to the dwarfs and said to them, "Give me the coffin, for I cannot live without Snow White. I will care for her coffin and keep her

always as my own." The dwarfs would take no gold, but when they saw that the king's son was suffering for his love of the girl, they had pity upon him and allowed his servants to carry the coffin off.

As they were traveling through the forest the servants stumbled over a tree stump. All at once the poisonous bit of apple that Snow White had eaten came up from her throat. A few moments later she opened her eyes and was once more alive. "Where am I?" she asked, looking about her.

"You are with me," said the king's son and he told her how it had come to pass. "Please stay with me and we shall be married. I love you more than anything on earth."

Snow White agreed and went with him to his father's palace. All the people from the king's land and the lands that bordered upon it were invited to the wedding feast, and among these was Snow White's stepmother.

When she had dressed herself in her most splendid gown, she went before the looking glass and said:

"Looking glass, looking glass, on the wall,
Who in the land is fairest of all?"

And the glass answered:

"Thou, Queen, are the fairest here I've seen,
But fairer still is the new-made queen."

When she heard this, the queen uttered a curse, but her envy and curiosity were so great that she went to the wedding feast to see her rival. And when she saw that it was Snow White, she stood rigid with rage and terror. But iron slippers had been heated in the fire, and now they were brought to the queen with tongs and set upon the stone floor. She was forced to wear the red-hot shoes, and danced and danced until she fell down dead.

PUSS IN BOOTS

Charles Perrault

Far out in the countryside there was a poor miller who died, leaving his three sons all that he owned. No lawyers were called in, as they would have taken everything; instead the sons divided the property among themselves. The eldest took the mill, the second the donkey, and the third was left with the miller's cat.

The youngest son was unhappy at having so poor a share. "My brothers can join together and earn a living," said he. "But once I have eaten my cat and made a muff from his skin, I will surely die of hunger."

The cat had been eavesdropping and now he decided to speak. "Do not fret, Master," he said in a respectful and serious tone. "Only give me a stout sack and a pair of boots to protect my feet from the brambles and you will find you have received the best portion of your father's estate."

Though the youth had little trust in the words of a cat, he had seen the creature play many clever tricks to snare rats and mice and so decided to give him what he asked.

The cat put on his boots and slung the sack around his neck. Then he went to a place he knew of, where many rabbits came to eat. He put a quantity of bran and some thistle leaves into his sack and stretched out near it as if he were a corpse. Soon a foolish young rabbit jumped into the sack and the cat pulled the drawstrings tight and killed him without mercy.

Proudly the cat took his prey to the palace and asked to speak with the king. He had decided that his master was to be

called the Marquis of Carabas, and when he was brought into the king's apartment, he bowed low, saying, "Look, sire, I have a rabbit that my noble lord, the Marquis of Carabas, has commanded me to present to you."

"Thank your master for me," said the king, "and tell him I am well pleased with his gift."

Another time the cat carried his sack and hid himself among some standing corn. When a brace of partridges ran into the sack, he drew the strings and so caught them both. Again he presented his prey to the king and again the king thanked him.

For two or three months the cat continued to bring his master's game to the king. One day, when he knew the king would be out along the riverside with his beautiful daughter, the cat said to his master, "If you will but follow my advice, your fortune shall be made. You must bathe in the river at a place I show you and then leave the rest to me."

The Marquis of Carabas went off to bathe without ever knowing why the cat wanted him to. But no sooner had he jumped into the water than the king passed by and the cat cried out loudly, "Help! Help! My lord, the Marquis of Carabas, is drowning!"

At this commotion the king looked out the window of his coach and recognized the cat who had so often brought him game. Quickly he commanded his guards to save his lordship, the Marquis of Carabas.

While they were drawing the marquis from the river, the cat came up to the coach and told the king his master's clothes had been stolen by some thieves, who had run off with them. But the cunning cat had hidden the clothing under a large stone. Quickly the king commanded a servant to hurry to the palace and fetch one of his own suits for the Marquis of Carabas.

When he was dressed, he looked fine and handsome and the king's daughter thought she liked him very much. Without the need of any instruction from his cat, the Marquis of Carabas treated her with affection and tenderness and soon she was quite in love with him.

The king invited the Marquis of Carabas to join them in their coach. The cat ran on before them, overjoyed that his scheme had begun to succeed. Coming upon some mowers who were scything a meadow, he said, "Good people, you must tell the king that the meadow you mow belongs to the Marquis of Carabas, or you shall be chopped into tiny pieces like herbs for the pot."

Then the king stopped his coach by the meadow and asked the mowers who owned it. "The Marquis of Carabas," they answered all together, for the cat's threat had made them afraid.

"You have a fine estate there," said the king to the Marquis of Carabas.

"Yes, sire," said the marquis quickly, "and it yields a plentiful harvest each year."

The cat, who went on before them, soon met some reapers. "Good people," he said, "if you do not say that the corn you are reaping belongs to the Marquis of Carabas, you shall be chopped as small as herbs for the pot."

The king when he passed asked the reapers who owned all the corn.

"The Marquis of Carabas," they answered at once.

The cat gave the same warning to all he met, and the king and his daughter were astonished at the vast estates of the Marquis of Carabas.

At last the cat came to a great castle that was commanded by an ogre, the richest ever known. All the lands that the king had passed through were part of the ogre's holdings. The cat had

taken care to learn everything he could about the ogre and now asked to see him, saying he had come to pay his respects.

The ogre received him as politely as an ogre could and made him sit down.

"I have been told," said the cat, "that you are able to change yourself into all sorts of creatures; that you can, for example, transform yourself into a lion."

"That is so," said the ogre roughly. "And just to convince you I shall now become a lion."

When he saw a huge lion so near, the cat became terrified and jumped up on the roof. His boots skidded and slipped upon the tiles and he nearly fell to his death. But when the ogre

became only an ogre once more, the cat came down and confessed to his fear.

"I have also been told," he said to the ogre, "that you can take the shape of tiny creatures; that you can, for example, transform yourself into a rat or even a mouse. But I must tell you I find this hard to believe."

"Hard to believe! You will soon see!" cried the ogre. And he changed himself into a mouse and began to scamper about on the floor. The cat lost no time, but fell upon him and ate him in one bite.

And now the king arrived at the ogre's castle and decided to stop there. The cat, who heard the coach pass over the drawbridge, ran outside and said to the king, "Welcome, Your Majesty, to the castle of the Marquis of Carabas."

"What! And does this castle too belong to you, my lord Marquis?" said the king. "Come, let us go inside."

Without a word the marquis gave his hand to the young princess and they followed the king. First they came into a great hall, where they found a splendid banquet the ogre had prepared for some friends. But the friends had seen the king's coach outside and so had not dared to enter.

Impressed by the vast wealth of the Marquis of Carabas and realizing his daughter was in love with him, the king said at last, "You will have only yourself to blame, my lord Marquis, if you are not soon my son-in-law."

The marquis bowed very low and accepted the honor the king had conferred upon him. That very same day he married the princess. The cat became a great lord and never again ran after mice except for the fun of it.

BEAUTY AND THE BEAST

Madame LePrince de Beaumont

Arich merchant in a far-off land had for many years been lucky in all his undertakings. His three daughters danced in jeweled ballgowns and his three sons rode Arabian steeds that moved like the wind.

Then one day for no reason the merchant suddenly lost everything. His house caught fire and burned to the ground, and all his ships at sea were sunk or plundered by pirates. Only a small country cottage remained to him, and the merchant was forced to move there with his children. The two older daughters grumbled continually, regretting the lost amusements of their past. But the youngest, who was called Beauty, tried her best to comfort her father and brothers.

After many months the merchant got news that one of his ships, which he believed was lost, had come safely into port. His children came to see him off on his journey to the harbor town,

naming the presents he must buy them. But Beauty did not ask for anything. When her father pressed her, she said she only wished for his safe return. "But surely, Beauty, there is some small treasure I may bring you," he said.

"If you see a rose along the way, you might pick it for me," she answered. "It is my favorite flower and it does not grow near here."

Then the merchant set out and reached the town. He soon discovered that his companions, believing him dead, had divided all the goods between them. Thus he was forced to return home, poorer even than when he had started.

The way led through a deep forest, and it was snowing so bitterly that his horse could hardly carry him farther. Just when the merchant was about to give up hope, he saw a track that opened into an avenue lined with orange trees. To his surprise no snow had fallen there and the air smelled sweet and warm.

Soon the merchant came to a courtyard and then he went inside a vast castle. He passed through many splendid rooms but no one answered when he called out. The place seemed entirely empty and a deep silence was everywhere. At last he saw a small sitting room where a cheerful fire was blazing. A table was set with all manner of wines and meats, and as the merchant was very hungry, he lost no time in beginning the meal. Afterward he looked again for his host to thank him but, finding no one, he lay down upon a couch before the fire and fell fast asleep.

When he awoke he was refreshed and ready to continue his journey. Just as he was passing out of the courtyard, he saw a hedge of roses. Remembering Beauty's request, he stopped and gathered one to bring to her. But no sooner had he done so than a hideous beast appeared. His face was so ugly that the man could not bear to look at it.

The beast spoke in a terrible voice. "So this, then, is how you show your gratitude? Was it not enough that I allowed you in my castle and was kind to you?"

The merchant fell to his knees. "Oh, please, noble beast, do not take my life. I only picked the rose for my daughter, Beauty, who begged me to get her one."

On hearing this, the beast said gruffly, "I will forgive you only if you send one of your daughters to die in your stead. She must come willingly or else I will not have her. Now you may stay and rest in my castle until tomorrow."

Although the merchant found an excellent supper laid for him, he could not eat; nor could he sleep, although everything had been provided for his comfort. The next morning he set out again on a fine horse that the beast had left him.

When he came near his house his children came out to greet him. But seeing the sadness in his face and his eyes filled with tears, they asked what was the matter. He gave Beauty the rose

and told her all that had happened. At once the two older sisters turned on Beauty. "It is your fault," they told her. "A rose indeed!"

"I shall go with Father," Beauty said. "We will keep his promise to the beast."

Her father and her brothers, who loved her, begged Beauty to change her mind, but nothing would sway her. Go she must, and so they set out the very next morning, riding together on the beast's horse. When they reached the avenue of orange trees, the statues were holding flaming torches and fireworks flared in the sky. The palace gates opened of themselves and Beauty and her father walked into a room where a delicious meal awaited them.

Hardly had they finished eating when they heard the beast's footsteps echoing on the marble floor. Beauty clung to her father in terror, but the beast spoke to them in a mild tone and inquired about their journey. "Have you come here willingly, Beauty, to die in place of your father?" he said at last.

"Yes, willingly, and I know that I must stay," she said, looking at his face and trying to keep her voice from trembling.

"That is good," the beast answered. "Your father may spend the night but must go home in the morning." He bowed and took his leave of them.

Beauty tried to comfort her father when they parted by saying that the beast did not seem very cruel. Perhaps he would relent and one day allow her to return home.

She watched him ride off and then walked up a curving stairway into a room with mirrors all around. On the door was written in golden letters "Beauty's Room," and in the mornings a clock awakened her by calling her name softly twelve times. She was alone all day but when she was having her supper the beast would draw the curtains and come in. He spoke to her so pleasantly that she soon lost much of her fear of him.

Each night just before he left, he turned toward her and said, "Am I very ugly?"

"Yes," replied Beauty, "but you are so kind to me that I no longer mind."

"Will you marry me then?" he asked.

"Pray do not ask me," said Beauty.

"Since you will not, then good night, Beauty." And the beast would go away.

The castle was full of galleries and apartments containing rare and precious things. In one room was a cage filled with exotic birds. In another a troop of monkeys of all sizes came to meet her, making low bows. Beauty was enchanted with them and asked the beast if she might have one to keep her company. At once two young apes appeared and two small monkeys with them. They chattered and jumped all around her, making Beauty laugh.

Each night at suppertime the beast came to see her. Gradually she came to know him and liked him more and more. But to his question, "Beauty, will you marry me?" she always said, "No, Beast," very gently. And when she said these words, it seemed to her that he was sad and in some way disappointed with her.

Though Beauty had everything she could wish for and was content there, she never stopped missing her father and her brothers and sisters. At last one evening she begged the beast to let her go home.

"Ah, Beauty, will you desert an unhappy beast so easily? Very well, then. You shall visit your home but must promise to return in two months' time. You will not need any horse to carry you back. Only take this ring and turn it twice upon your finger the night before you come away and in the morning you will be with me."

The beast told her to take all that she wanted from the castle as presents for her family and he gave her two trunks. Though Beauty heaped them to the top with gold and trinkets, there always seemed to be more room, and they were not filled until she was tired of packing them. She went to sleep, but in the morning when she awoke she was in a strange place. Suddenly she heard her father's voice and knew that she was home.

Her sisters and brothers greeted her joyfully. But though their fortunes had changed and they were living in the town again, their entertainments seemed hollow and Beauty often

thought of the castle, where she had been so happy. As the weeks went by she spoke of returning, but her father and brothers begged her to stay and she had not the courage to say goodbye to them.

The ring the beast had given her was on her dressing stand and one night Beauty put it on and gazed into the stone. Slowly an image appeared and she saw the beast in a far part of the castle gardens. He was lying on his back and seemed to be dying. In a panic Beauty grasped the ring and turned it around two times.

In the morning she was at the beast's castle. She searched everywhere but could not find him. At last she ran to the place in the gardens she had dreamed of and came upon the beast lying among the high bushes. Beauty put her head down on his chest but at first he was not breathing. Then she began to weep. "Oh, he is dead and it is on my account," she said, and her tears fell upon his face.

Slowly the beast opened his eyes.

"Oh, Beast, how you frightened me!" Beauty cried. "I never before knew how much I loved you."

"Can you really care for such an ugly creature as I am?" said the beast faintly.

"Yes, oh yes, dear Beast. Only live to be my husband and I will be your wife forever."

The moment Beauty uttered these words, a dazzling light shone everywhere. The palace windows glittered with lamps, and music was heard all around. To Beauty's great wonder a handsome prince stood before her. He said that her words had broken the spell of a magician, who had doomed him to wear the form of a beast. This terrible enchantment could be broken only when a maiden loved him in spite of his ugliness.

Then the grateful prince claimed Beauty as his bride. Her family was sent for and the wedding was celebrated the very next day.

THE FROG PRINCE

The Brothers Grimm

In olden times, when wishing was still of some use, there lived a king whose daughters were all beautiful. But the youngest was so very beautiful that the sun itself was amazed each time it shone upon her face.

Close to the king's castle was a large, dark forest where an old lime tree with spreading branches grew. Beneath the tree was a fountain. Whenever the day was hot, the king's child would run there to play, taking with her a golden ball. Over and over she threw it up and caught it, and this ball was her favorite toy.

Now one day it happened that the golden ball did not fall back into her hand, but rolled over the rim of the fountain. The king's daughter followed the ball with her eyes, but it sank slowly and vanished beneath the clouded water. Then the girl began to weep, and her tears came harder and harder. She thought she was all alone, but suddenly she heard a voice: "Why are you weeping, king's daughter? Your tears would melt even a stone to pity."

She looked around and saw a frog stretching his thick, ugly head from the water. "Ah, water paddler, so it was you that spoke!" she said. "I am weeping for my golden ball, which has slipped away from me into the fountain."

"Listen, then, and do not weep," answered the frog. "I will fetch your plaything up again, but you must give me something in return."

"What will you have, dear frog?" she said. "Perhaps my pearls and jewels? Or do you want my golden crown?"

"I care nothing for wealth," the frog answered. "But if you will love me and let me be your companion, and sit at your table, and eat from your plate, and sleep in your little bed—if you will promise me all these things, then I will dive down into the water after your golden ball."

"Yes, yes, I promise!" she said. But she thought to herself, "What is the silly frog saying? Let him stay in the water with the other frogs. He can never be my companion."

The frog had heard only the promise and not the thought. At once he plunged his head into the water, kicking hard with his legs. Down, down, down he swam, then came up again with the golden ball and threw it on the grass. With a cry of delight, the king's daughter took her beautiful plaything and ran off through the forest.

"Stop! Stop!" cried the frog. "Take me with you. I cannot run as you can!" But all his croaking was of no use, for the king's daughter never listened.

The next evening, when she was sitting at the table with her father and all his courtiers, something came creeping, *splish splash, splish splash,* up the marble stairs. At the top it knocked upon the door and cried, "Let me in, youngest princess. Let me in."

So she rose to see who had called her. When she opened the door, there sat the frog. Her heart began to beat violently and she slammed the door shut and returned to the table. The king saw that she was frightened and asked her if perhaps a giant had come to fetch her away.

"Oh, no," she answered. "It is no giant, but a horrid frog."

"And what does he want with you?" asked the king.

"Ah, dear Father, yesterday when I was playing near the fountain, my golden ball fell into the water. I cried so much that the frog carried it up again. But first, because he asked me, I promised he could be my companion. I never thought he would leave the fountain, but somehow he has jumped out and now he wants to come in here."

Then the king said, "What you have promised you must fulfill. Go at once and let him in." So the girl went and opened the door. Then the frog hopped in and followed her, step by step, to her chair.

"Lift me up," he croaked. "I am not so large as you are."

She delayed and delayed until the king commanded her to do it. Once the frog was on the chair, he wanted to be on the table, and once he was on the table, he wanted to eat from her golden plate. "Push it close to me," he said, "so that we might share the food between us."

The girl could not eat a mouthful, but the frog finished everything. At last he said, "I am tired now. Carry me to your room and then we will sleep in your silken bed."

She began to cry, for she was frightened of the cold, ugly creature who was now to share her bed. But the king was angry and said, "He who helped you when you were in trouble must not now be despised."

So the girl took the frog up with two fingers and put him in a corner of her room. But as she lay in her bed, he crept up to it. "Put me on the pillow beside you, or I will tell your father," said he.

No longer could she bear it! Catching hold of the frog, she threw him with all her might against the wall. "Now, will you be quiet, you ugly frog!" she screamed.

But at the moment he fell, he was changed from a frog into a prince. He told her he had been under the spell of an evil witch and that only a king's youngest daughter had the power to rescue him from the fountain.

Her father had said he must be her companion. Now that he was a prince she wanted to marry him and he could hardly refuse. They were soon betrothed and the next morning, when the sun rose, a carriage drawn by eight white horses came up to the palace. Behind it stood Faithful Henry, the servant of the prince. When his master was changed into a frog, Faithful Henry had grieved so hard that he had bound three iron bands around his heart for fear that it would break. But now the prince was saved and they were to return to his own kingdom.

Faithful Henry helped the bride and bridegroom into the

carriage and sat down on the seat behind. They had not gone far when the prince heard a crack as if something had broken. "Henry, the carriage is breaking," said he.

"No, Master, it is not the carriage, but a band around my heart that was put there to keep it from breaking when you were bewitched."

Twice again along the journey there was the same cracking sound, and each time the prince thought some part of the carriage had given way. But it was only the breaking of the last bonds around Faithful Henry's heart. Now that the prince was set free, his servant had no more need of them.

THE VALIANT LITTLE TAILOR

The Brothers Grimm

One fine summer morning a little tailor was sewing at his window. The streets were quiet, and then from far away he heard a farmer's wife call out, "Jam for sale! Sweet jam for sale!"

It sounded good to the tailor, so he leaned out the window and said, "Come here, old woman. This is the place you will sell your wares."

She walked up the three steps to the tailor's shop with her heavy basket and showed him what she had. "Ah, delicious," the tailor said. "I will take four ounces. And if it is a quarter of a pound, that makes no difference to me." The woman, who had hoped for a much better sale, gave him what he asked for but went away grumbling.

The tailor never noticed. He took some bread from his cupboard, cut a large piece, and spread the jam over it. "This is just what I need," said he. "It will give me strength for my work. Oh, but before I eat I must finish this jacket." So he put the bread on a chair nearby and sewed away, making larger and larger stitches because he was so excited.

In the meantime the sweet smell of jam rose up toward the ceiling and attracted a number of flies.

"What's this? Who asked you to have a taste?" cried the tailor, waving the uninvited guests away.

But it was no use. The flies did not understand his words,

and they returned and kept returning. At last the tailor became angry. He took a piece of cloth and slapped it at the flies, crying, "Now you'll see what I have for you!"

When he was done he counted no fewer than seven of them lying dead. The tailor was amazed at his own skill and bravery. In great haste he cut out a belt and stitched the words "Seven at one blow" upon it. "The whole town must hear of this!" he exclaimed. "What? Not just the town! The whole world will know!" Then the little tailor buckled the belt around his waist and prepared to go out into the world.

In the cupboard he found some old cheese, which he stuck in his pocket. And as he was walking through the door, he saw a bird caught in a thicket. This too went into his pocket with the cheese. Now the tailor was ready and he set out on his journey, filled with excitement and curiosity.

The road led up a high mountain. When he reached the top he saw an enormous giant sitting peacefully. The little tailor did not hesitate but went straight up to him and said, "Good morning, my friend. You have a fine view. As for me, I am traveling the world in search of adventure. Would you like to come?"

The giant looked at the little tailor with contempt. "You miserable runt! Why, I could crush you with my big toe."

"Stop!" cried the tailor. "Not so fast! I know I am not large; however . . ." He unbuttoned his coat and pointed to the words on his belt. "If you can read, that will show you what kind of man I am."

The giant read "Seven at one blow" and, thinking it must be seven men that the tailor had killed, began to feel more respect for him. Perhaps the little fellow was worthy of a challenge. "Can you do this?" the giant asked. As the tailor watched, he took a large stone and squeezed it until water ran from it.

"Oh, that is nothing," said the tailor. "It's quite simple, really." Then he brought from his pocket the soft cheese and squeezed it until the whey came out. "You see," he told the giant. "I can even draw milk from a stone. Beat that, I ask you!"

The giant did not know what to say. The strength of the little tailor quite amazed him. But he was not going to be bested in the contest, so he took another stone and threw it into the air. Up and up it went, so high that the eye could scarcely follow it. "Now, little man, let's see what you can do!" cried the giant.

"I'll admit the throw was a good one," said the tailor. "But after all the stone will fall down somewhere. Watch carefully and you will see that the stone I throw will disappear." Then he put his hand into his pocket, took out the bird, and threw it upward with all his might. At once the bird spread its wings and vanished in the air. "Now what do you think of that?" said the tailor modestly.

"Well," the giant admitted, "you can certainly throw. But

can you carry? That is what we'll have to find out." He led the tailor to a great oak that had fallen on the ground. "Now, if you are as strong as you say, help me carry this tree out of the forest."

"Willingly," replied the tailor. "You must take the trunk on your shoulders and I will carry the leaves and branches, as they are by far the larger part."

With much panting and heaving the giant took the trunk on his shoulders, but the clever tailor only sat among the branches. In this way the giant, who could not look behind him, carried the whole tree and the tailor besides. Soon he was forced to stop. "The load is too heavy. I shall have to let it fall."

At once the tailor sprang down and seized the tree with both hands as if he had been carrying it.

They went on together until they came to a cherry tree laden with ripe fruit. The giant seized the highest branch, bent it down, and gave it to the tailor. "Eat," he said. "Have as much fruit as you like."

But as soon as the giant let go of the branch, it sprang up again, flinging the tailor into the air as if it were a slingshot. The giant laughed and laughed. "Look at you! You can't even hang on to a twig."

"Do you imagine a man who could kill seven at one blow would falter at such a simple task?" said the tailor. "No, I jumped over the tree because I saw hunters shooting in the forest nearby. Now you do the same; you jump over the tree."

The giant tried but only got tangled in the branches, so again the tailor had the upper hand.

Then the giant said to him, "Since you are such a valiant fellow, you'd better come with me to my cave and spend the night."

The little tailor agreed, but when they reached the cavern, there sat two other giants before a blazing fire. "Never would I have imagined such a thing," thought the tailor. "The world is a fascinating place."

After giving him a leg of mutton, the giant showed the little tailor the bed where he was to sleep. But it was not comfortable, so the tailor crept into a corner and put his coat under his head for a pillow.

At midnight the giant, thinking the tailor was fast asleep in the bed, rose up and struck a blow across it with a heavy iron bar. "Ah, there's an end to the cunning little grasshopper. And about time too."

But the next morning, when the giants were out in the forest

not even thinking of the tailor, he walked up to them as boldly as ever. The giants thought he had come to life again and were so terrified that they took to their heels and ran off screaming.

The little tailor continued on his way, always following his nose. Finally he came into the courtyard of a king's palace. As he felt weary, he lay down on the grass and was soon fast asleep.

While he lay there the people passing by read the words on his belt. "Seven at one blow!" they exclaimed. "We must go and tell the king."

Though it was a time of peace, the king was eager to engage the services of such a great warrior. He sent an ambassador out to tell him so. The man waited until the tailor opened his eyes and stretched his limbs, and then he delivered the king's message.

"To serve the king, you say?" answered the tailor. "Why, that is the very reason I have come."

He was received at the palace with honor and given lavish apartments for his use. But the king's soldiers were jealous of the little tailor and they went before His Majesty. "We want nothing to do with a man who can kill seven at one blow. We will never fight alongside him."

The king did not wish to lose all his soldiers for the sake of one and began to wish he'd never set eyes on the little tailor. But like the others he was afraid to anger a man who had killed seven at one blow.

At last he sent for the tailor and said, "In a forest not far from here two giants dwell. They plunder and murder and loot and no one can subdue them. You may have one hundred soldiers for an escort, and if you kill the giants I will give you my daughter for a wife and half my kingdom in the bargain."

"This is a prize worth trying for," thought the little tailor. "It does not come every day to a man like me." So he said to the king, "Yes, sire, I will destroy the giants but I do not need your hundred soldiers. I who have killed seven at one blow am not likely to be afraid of two."

The tailor set out with the soldiers following, but when they reached the boundary of the forest he told them to wait, as he would rather go alone to attack the giants.

He walked among the trees and soon saw them, fast asleep

and snoring. The little tailor gathered a pocketful of stones and climbed the hemlock under which they slept. Taking careful aim, he dropped one stone after another onto the chest of the larger giant.

The giant awoke with a roar and pushed his companion roughly. "What do you mean, pelting me with stones?" he yelled.

"You are dreaming," said the other. "I never touched you!" They argued about it for a time and fell back to sleep.

Now the tailor was ready again. He took the heaviest stone in his pocket and dropped it right on the chest of the smaller giant. At once the giant woke up and cried in rage, "Now it's you who are pelting me!"

"I never did!" said the larger giant.

"What! Are you saying I'm a liar?" roared the other. Then he sprang up in a fury and knocked his companion against the hemlock until its branches nearly shattered.

The other returned his blows and soon the two giants were locked in combat. So violently did they fight that they uprooted the trees all around them and the earth shook under their feet. Finally they both lay dead.

Down jumped the little tailor and walked out of the forest unharmed. "It is over," he said to the king's soldiers. "The giants struggled against me and rooted up the very trees for weapons, but all this was useless against a man who has killed seven at one blow."

The tailor then returned to the palace and went before the king to claim the princess and half the kingdom. But the king was not willing to keep his promise. "There is one more thing you must do for me," he told the tailor. "In my forests a fierce unicorn lives. Long has he terrorized the countryside and many are those he has killed. Now you must catch him and bring him to me."

"One unicorn will be nothing after two giants," the tailor

answered. He went into the forests, again asking those who had accompanied him to remain behind. Carrying only a rope and an axe, he approached the unicorn. The animal pawed the ground and prepared to strike, but the little tailor jumped quickly behind a tree. "Softly, softly," he cried. "There is no need for haste."

At this the unicorn charged, ramming his horn so hard into the tree trunk that it stuck fast.

"Now I have got my bird," said the tailor. He put the rope around the unicorn's neck, cut the horn out of the tree with his axe, and led the animal back to the king.

But even now the king was not willing to grant the prize. "Before you marry my daughter," he told the tailor, "you must catch a wild boar that is tearing up all my meadowland."

Once again the soldiers were sent with him and once again the little tailor refused their help and bade them wait at the boundary.

As soon as the wild boar caught sight of the tailor, he flew at the tailor with his tusks gleaming. But the tailor was too quick. He sprang into a little chapel that stood nearby and then jumped out through a window. The boar only saw him enter and so followed him in and raced about in circles. Then the tailor bolted the door, trapped the animal easily, and presented him to the king.

Whether he liked it or not the king was at last obliged to keep his promise. The wedding took place with great pomp but little rejoicing and thus was a tailor made into a king.

Some time later the young queen heard her husband talking in his sleep. "Work away, there's a good lad," he was saying. "Finish that coat and sew the seams of the trousers or I shall box your ears."

The next morning she told her father that he had married her to a tailor and not a hero. She wept and moaned and begged him to help her get rid of her husband.

"Listen closely," said the king. "Tonight you must leave your bedroom door unlocked and my servants will stand outside. When the tailor has fallen asleep, they will tie him up and carry him on board a ship that is soon to set sail."

But one of the servants close to the little tailor told him of the plot. When night came and the queen was lying beside him, he tossed and turned and pretended to cry out in his sleep. "Be quick, lad. Finish that coat and sew the seams of the trousers or I shall box your ears. I have killed seven at one blow; I have destroyed two giants; I have hunted a unicorn and taken a wild boar captive. Shall I be afraid of those who stand waiting outside my bedroom door?"

When the servants heard this, they were terrified and fled as if all those whom the tailor had killed were after them. From that time no one in the kingdom dared to plot against him, and so the little tailor remained a king for the rest of his days.

RED RIDING HOOD

The Brothers Grimm

Long ago there lived a little girl who was loved by all who knew her, but she was especially dear to her grandmother. The woman would do anything to make the child happy, and once she gave her a soft red velvet cloak. It was so very pretty that from that day on the girl would wear nothing else, and she came to be called Red Riding Hood.

One day her mother said to her, "Come here, Red Riding Hood, and carry this cake and a bottle of wine to Grandmother. She is ill and will be glad to have them. Go quickly before the sun is high, and do not daydream or wander about in the forest. When you come into Grandmother's room, you must curtsy and wish her good morning."

"I will do just as you say," Red Riding Hood promised.

Her grandmother lived a good distance from the village in the midst of the forest. When Red Riding Hood came to the edge of the forest, she met a wolf. The child did not know that he was a wicked animal and so she was not at all afraid of him.

"Good morning, Red Riding Hood," he said.

"Good morning, Wolf."

"And where are you going so early, Red Riding Hood?"

"To Grandmother's."

"What is that in your basket?"

"A cake and some wine. I'm taking it to Grandmother. She is ill and wants something to make her stronger."

"Where does your grandmother live, Red Riding Hood?"

"Down this path and into the forest. Her house stands beneath three big oak trees, near a hedge of chestnuts. Surely you must know it," said Red Riding Hood.

The wolf looked her up and down and thought to himself, "This tender young child will be a juicy morsel, even nicer than the old woman. If I am clever, I shall be able to snap them both up."

He walked along with Red Riding Hood for a time. Then he said, "Look at all the flowers, Red Riding Hood. Why don't you look about you? I think you do not even hear the birds sing. You are just as solemn as if you were going to school, but everything is so gay out here in the woods."

Red Riding Hood raised her eyes, and when she saw the sunlight dancing through the trees and the bright flowers, she thought, "Suppose I pick a bouquet for Grandmother—that would please her. And it is still quite early."

So she left the path and wandered off among the trees to pick the flowers. Each time she picked one, she saw another, more beautiful, farther on. In this way she went deeper and deeper into the forest and the sun rose high in the sky.

After he left Red Riding Hood, the wolf went straight to the grandmother's house and knocked at the door.

"Who is there?"

"It is Red Riding Hood, bringing you a cake and some wine. Open the door!"

"Lift the latch," cried the old woman. "I am too weak to get up."

The wolf lifted the latch, and the door sprang open. He went straight in without saying a word and ate up the old woman. Then he put on her nightgown and nightcap, climbed into the bed, and drew the curtains.

Red Riding Hood ran about picking flowers until she could carry no more, and then she remembered her grandmother again. When she got to the cottage she was astonished to find the door open, and when she went into the room everything seemed strange.

She felt very frightened, but she did not know why. "Good morning, Grandmother," she cried, but she heard no answer.

Then she went up to the bed and drew the curtains. There lay her grandmother, but she had pulled her cap down over her face and looked very odd.

"Oh, Grandmother, what big ears you have!" she said.

"The better to hear you with, my dear."

"Grandmother, what big eyes you have!"

"The better to see you with, my dear."

"What big hands you have, Grandmother!"

"The better to catch hold of you, my dear."

"But, Grandmother, what big teeth you have."

"The better to eat you with, my dear!" Then the wolf sprang out of bed, rushed at Little Red Riding Hood, and de-voured her in one mouthful. With his belly full, the wolf went

back to bed and soon he was snoring loudly.

Some time later a huntsman passed by the house and heard a fearful racket. "How loudly the old woman is snoring," he thought. "I must see if there is something the matter with her."

So he went inside and up to the bed, where he found the wolf fast asleep. "Is it really you, you old rascal?" he said. "Long enough have I sought you."

He raised up his gun to shoot, then suddenly thought that perhaps the wolf had eaten up the old lady, and she might still be saved. So he took a knife and began to cut open the sleeping wolf. At his first cut he saw the red cloak, and after a few more slashes, the little girl sprang out. "Oh, how frightened I was! It was so dark and close inside the wolf!" she cried. Next the grandmother came out. She was still alive, but hardly able to breathe.

The huntsman told Red Riding Hood to bring some big stones. Then they filled the wolf's belly with them and sewed him up. When the wolf awoke and tried to run away, the stones dragged him back and he fell down dead at last.

They were all joyful now. The huntsman skinned the wolf and took away the skin. The grandmother ate the cake and drank the wine Red Riding Hood had brought, and soon was stronger. And as for Red Riding Hood, she knew now that she must listen to her mother and never wander off in the forest again.

THE REAL PRINCESS
(THE PRINCESS AND THE PEA)
Hans Christian Andersen

There was once a prince and he wanted a princess, but she had to be a real princess. He traveled through the world to find one, but always something seemed to be wrong. Though many he met claimed to be real princesses, he could never be sure that this was true. At last he returned home and he was very sad because he wanted a real princess so badly.

One evening a terrible storm came up. Lightning flashed in the sky and rain tore at the castle walls. It was a dark and fearful night. Then in the midst of the storm a knock came at the city gates. The old king himself went to open them.

A princess stood outside, but the storm had left her in a terrible state. Water streamed from her hair and her clothes; it ran in at the toes of her shoes and out at the heels; but still she said she was a real princess.

"Well, we shall soon discover if that is true," thought the old queen, but she said nothing. She went into the bedroom, took all the bedclothes off, and laid a pea on the bottom boards of the bed. Then she took twenty mattresses and piled them on top of the pea, and then she put twenty feather beds on top of the mattresses. This is where the princess was to spend the night.

In the morning the queen, the king, and the prince came into the room and asked the princess how she had slept.

"Oh, it was dreadful!" said the princess. "I hardly closed my eyes the whole night. I don't know what it could have been, but I was lying on something so hard that my whole body is black and blue."

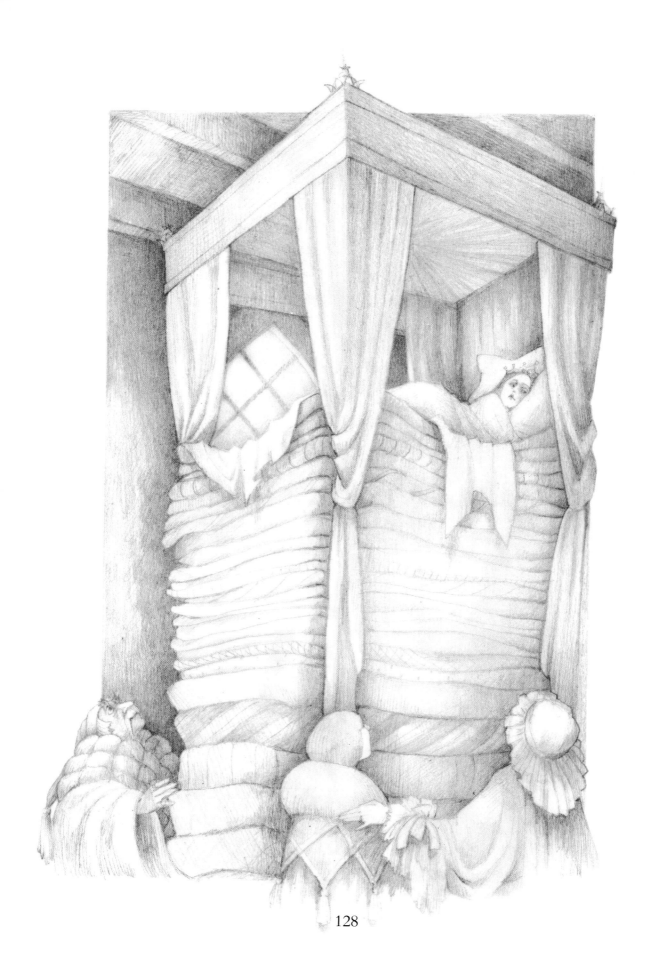

Then they saw at once that she must be a real princess, for she had felt the pea through twenty mattresses and twenty feather beds. Nobody but a real princess would have such delicate skin.

So the prince took her for a wife because now he knew he had at last found a real princess. And as for the pea, that was put into a museum, where it may still be seen if no one has taken it.

Now isn't this a real story?

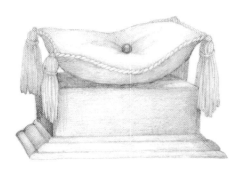

THE STEADFAST TIN SOLDIER

Hans Christian Andersen

Once upon a time there were five and twenty tin soldiers. They were all brothers, for they had been made from the same tin spoon. As soon as the lid was taken off their box, they heard someone cry, "Soldiers! Soldiers!" and then a little boy drew them out one by one and set them upon a table. It was his birthday and they had been given to him for a present.

Each man shouldered his gun and kept his eyes face front. They looked very handsome in their shiny red uniforms, but one was a little different from the others. He had only one leg, for he had been made last and the tin had run out. Yet there he stood, as steadfast on one leg as the others were on two, and he is the hero of this story.

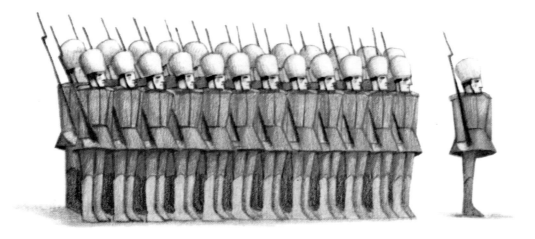

On the table with the tin soldiers were many other toys. The most wonderful of all was a paper castle with tiny windows and perfect, miniature rooms inside. It was surrounded by small trees and there was even a looking-glass lake with wax swans swimming upon it.

A beautiful maiden stood at the door of the castle. She too had been cut from paper, but she wore a gauze dress and a little blue ribbon fastened with a brilliant spangle nearly the size of her face. The maiden held both her arms outstretched, for she was a dancer, and one of her legs was raised high in the air. From his place on the table the tin soldier couldn't see it at all and so he supposed that she, like himself, had only one leg.

"That is the wife for me!" he thought. "But she is much too grand. How can I offer her a box with five and twenty tin soldiers when she has a castle for her home?" Yet he could not take his eyes off the little dancer, who stood upon one leg without ever losing her balance.

Late in the evening, when the people of the house went to bed, the toys began to play. They paid visits to one another and fought battles and gave balls. The nutcrackers turned somersaults and the pencil scribbled on the slate. Even the canary in his cage woke up and began to sing. Only the tin soldier and the little dancer did not move. While the other toys romped and chattered, they stood quietly, each upon one leg, dreaming their separate dreams.

Then the clock struck twelve and the lid of the snuff box popped up. Inside was a little black goblin, a sort of jack-in-the-box.

"Tin soldier!" said the goblin. "Why are you staring at the dancer? Keep your eyes to yourself!"

But the tin soldier pretended not to hear.

"I am warning you. Just wait until tomorrow!" said the goblin.

In the morning, when the children woke up, they put the tin soldier on the windowsill. Perhaps it was the wind or perhaps it was the goblin, but all at once the window flew open and the tin soldier fell headfirst three stories to the ground.

It was a terrific descent and at last he landed with his leg in the air and his bayonet caught between two paving stones. The little boy and the maidservant ran down to look for him, but though they almost stepped on the tin soldier, they never saw him. "Here I am," he could have shouted to alert them, but he felt it would be wrong to ask for help when he was in uniform.

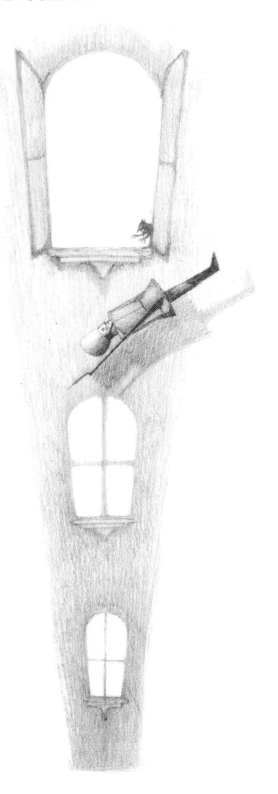

Presently it began to rain and the drops fell faster and faster until the lawns and streets were flooded. When the storm ended, two street urchins wandered by.

"Look, a tin soldier!" said one. "Let's take him sailing."

So they made a boat out of a newspaper and set the soldier in the middle of it. Away he sailed down the gutter while the two boys ran alongside clapping their hands. The waves rocked the boat wildly and the current whirled it around like a top. A shudder went through the tin soldier, but he only held his bayonet more firmly and looked straight ahead. Suddenly the boat sailed into a long wooden tunnel and everything was dark.

"Where am I going to now?" he thought. "I'll bet it's the fault of that goblin. But, oh, if the little dancer were here in the boat, the darkness would mean nothing to me."

At this moment a big water rat, who lived in the tunnel, came up. "Have you a pass?" he asked. "Hand over your pass."

The tin soldier did not speak, but clung even more tightly to his gun. The paper boat rushed on with the rat close behind. The rat gnashed his teeth and shouted loudly, "Stop him! Stop

him! He hasn't paid his toll. He hasn't shown his pass." The words echoed from the walls of the tunnel but no one was there.

The current grew stronger and stronger, and now the tin soldier saw daylight before him and heard a roaring, rushing sound. Imagine his terror! At the end of the tunnel was a great canal and there was nothing to grab on to, no way to stop the boat at all.

It swirled around three or four times and filled with water to the rim. The tin soldier never winced but stood proud and erect, and the paper boat sank deeper and deeper. Just before the water closed over his head, he thought of the pretty little dancer, whom he was never to see again. A song he had once heard rang in his ears:

Onward, onward, soldier,
For death is drawing near.

Then the paper boat came apart and the tin soldier fell through into the canal. Instantly he was swallowed by a big fish.

How narrow and dark it was inside the fish! But the tin

soldier was as steadfast as ever. He lay there full length, shouldering his gun and waiting to see what was to become of him.

The fish writhed back and forth, throwing its tail about. Then suddenly it became very quiet. A flash like lightning pierced through and the soldier saw broad daylight. "Well, look who's here," someone called loudly. "A tin soldier." The fish had been caught, taken to market, and sold. And now it was in the kitchen, where the cook had cut it open with a knife. She took the soldier up by the waist and carried him into the parlor, where everyone wanted to see the wonderful man who had traveled about in a fish.

They set him up on the table, and as he looked around he saw that he was in the very same room he had been in before. There were the children and the same toys standing upon the table. There was the beautiful castle with the little dancer in the doorway.

She still balanced upon one leg and held the other high in the air, for she too was steadfast. The soldier was moved and would have wept tears of tin if he had not been in uniform. He looked at her and she looked at him, but they said nothing.

At that very moment one of the little boys snatched up the tin soldier and threw him into the fire. There was no reason why he should have done such a thing. Perhaps the goblin in the snuff box was to blame.

The tin soldier stood there all lit up by the flames. The heat was terrible; perhaps it came from the real fire or perhaps it was from love. He had lost his bright colors, but whether it was from the journey or from his sorrow, nobody could tell.

He looked at the little dancer and she looked at him, and he felt himself melting away, but still he stood steadfast and shouldered his gun bravely. Then suddenly a door opened, the wind caught the little dancer, and she flew like a snowflake straight into the fire. She touched the tin soldier for an instant and then blazed up in flames.

The next day, when the maidservant came to take away the ashes, she found the tin soldier melted in the shape of a small tin heart. Of the dancer nothing remained but her spangle, burned black and shiny as coal.

CINDERELLA

Charles Perrault

There once was a man whose wife died and so he took another. The new wife was proud and haughty, and had two daughters who were just like her in every way. But the man also had a daughter, and she was sweet and gentle and good as gold.

The wedding was hardly over before the woman began to make her stepdaughter's life a misery. The young girl's goodness was like a beacon showing up the faults of her own two daughters and so the woman could not bear her. She gave the girl the meanest work in the house to do. She had to scour the dishes and scrub the floors and pick up after her stepsisters.

From early morning until late at night she was made to work, and her bedroom was in a garret way at the top of the house. She slept upon a wretched straw bed while her two stepsisters lay in fine rooms with carpets on the floors and looking glasses so tall that they could see themselves from head to foot. The young girl did all she was asked and dared not complain to her father, who would only have scolded her, for his new wife ruled him entirely.

When she had finished her work, she used to go into the chimney corner and sit quietly among the cinders, and so she was called Cinderwench. But the younger sister, who was not quite so rude as the others, called her Cinderella. In her ragged clothing, with her dirty face, Cinderella was yet a hundred times more beautiful than her stepsisters.

After some months had passed, the king's son gave a ball for all the stylish people in the countryside. The two sisters were

also invited and immediately they set about choosing the gowns and petticoats, the hair ornaments and slippers they would wear. This made Cinderella's work still harder, for it was she who ironed their linen and pleated their ruffles. All day long the sisters talked of nothing but how they should be dressed.

"I think I shall wear my red velvet suit with the French trimmings," said the eldest.

"And I," said the youngest, "shall wear my gold-flowered mantle and my diamond necklace."

The best hairdressers were called in to style their hair; the best face powder and lip rouge were obtained. In all these matters the sisters consulted Cinderella, for she always knew what was most becoming. One night, as she was helping them to undress, they said to her, "Cinderella, would you not like to go to the ball?"

"Please, sisters, do not mock me," she said. "How could I ever dream of such a thing?"

"You are right," they answered. "People would surely laugh to see a Cinderwench at the ball."

For two days the sisters could hardly eat for excitement. So tightly did they lace themselves that they broke a dozen laces, and they were always at their looking glasses, trying on their gowns.

At last the evening of the ball came. Cinderella watched the sisters leave for the court, and when she had lost sight of them, she began to weep.

Her godmother, who was a fairy, saw her tears and asked what was the matter.

"I wish I could— I wish I could—" But she could not speak for crying.

"You wish you could go to the ball. Is that not so?" said her godmother.

Cinderella nodded with her eyes cast down.

"Well, then, go you shall," said her godmother. Then she took the girl and bade her go into the garden for a pumpkin.

Cinderella picked the finest she could find and carried it back to her godmother, though she could not imagine how a pumpkin could help her get to the ball. Then her godmother scooped out the inside of it, leaving nothing but the rind, and struck it with her wand. Instantly the pumpkin turned into a fine gilded coach.

Next her godmother went to look in the mousetrap, where she found six mice, all alive. She told Cinderella to lift the trap door, and as each mouse came out she tapped it with her wand. One by one the mice were turned into dapple-gray horses, and soon there was a fine set of them to draw the coach.

But they would still need a coachman, so Cinderella said, "I will go and see if there isn't a rat in the rat trap. Perhaps we might make a coachman of him."

"You are right," replied her godmother. "Go quickly and look."

Cinderella brought the rat trap to her and there were three rats inside. The godmother chose the one with the longest whiskers, and as soon as she touched him with her wand he became a fat coachman with a most imposing beard.

After that she said to Cinderella, "Go again into the garden and you will find six lizards behind the watering pot. Bring them to me by their tails."

As soon as the girl had done so, her godmother turned them into six footmen, who jumped up behind the coach and held on as if they had done nothing else their whole lives.

Then her godmother said to Cinderella, "Well, my dear, here is your carriage. I hope it pleases you."

"Oh, yes!" the girl cried. "But am I to wear these rags to the ball?"

Her godmother simply touched Cinderella with her wand

and at once her clothes were turned into a gown of gold and silver with jewels embroidered on the skirt. Then she gave Cinderella a pair of glass slippers, the most beautiful imaginable. But as the girl was making ready to leave, her godmother warned her that she must return home by midnight. If she stayed one moment longer, her coach would be a pumpkin again, her horses mice, her coachman a rat, her footmen lizards, and her clothing would turn back into rags.

Cinderella promised she would not be late and then she went off to the ball, her heart pounding for joy.

The king's son had been told that a great princess, unknown to all the company, would soon arrive, and he ran out to receive her himself. He gave her his hand as she sprang from the coach and led her into the hall where everyone was assembled. At once there was silence. So awed were the guests by the mysterious princess that they left off dancing and the musicians ceased to play. Then a hushed murmur swept the room:

"Ah, how lovely she is! How lovely!"

The king himself, old as he was, could not keep his eyes off her, and he whispered to the queen that he had never before seen a more enchanting creature.

All the women looked closely at her gown and her hair ornaments so they might have theirs made to the same pattern, if only they could find such fine silk and jewels, and such skillful hands to work them.

The king's son led her across the floor and they danced together again and again. A fine banquet was served, but the young prince only gazed at her and could not eat a bite.

After a time she left his side and went to sit by her sisters. She treated them with kindness and offered them sections of the oranges that the prince had given her. It very much pleased them to be singled out in this way.

Then Cinderella heard the clock strike a quarter to twelve. Quickly she wished the company good night and ran from the hall and down the palace steps to her coach.

When she was home again she found her godmother and thanked her and asked if she might go to the ball again the next day. As she was telling her godmother all that had happened, her two sisters came into the room.

"How long you have stayed!" she greeted them, rubbing her eyes as if she had been asleep.

"You would have stayed as well," said her sisters. "There was an unknown princess, the most beautiful ever seen in this world. She sat with us and gave us oranges."

"Was she really so very beautiful? And do you not know her name?" Then Cinderella turned to the eldest one. "Ah, dear sister, won't you give me your yellow dress that you wear every day so that I might see the princess for myself?"

"Lend my clothing to a dirty Cinderwench? I should be out of my mind!" cried the sister.

Cinderella had expected such an answer and she was very glad of the refusal. The next evening the two sisters went to the ball and she went too, dressed even more exquisitely than the first time. The king's son was always with her and spoke to her with words of praise. So entranced was Cinderella that she forgot her godmother's warning and heard the chimes of midnight when she thought it could be no more than eleven o'clock.

At once she arose and fled, nimble as a deer. Though the prince rushed after her, he could not catch her. In her haste she left behind one of the glass slippers, which he picked up and carried with him.

Cinderella's coach had vanished and she had to run home in the dark. Of her finery nothing remained but the other glass slipper. The guards at the palace gates were asked if they had

seen a princess, but they replied that no one had come there but a poor country girl dressed all in rags.

When the two sisters returned from the ball, Cinderella asked them if they had enjoyed it and whether the unknown princess had again appeared. They told her yes, but said she had hurried away the moment the clock struck midnight. And now the king's son had only the glass slipper she had left behind. They said he was brokenhearted and would do anything to find her once more.

All of this was true. A few days afterward the king's son proclaimed that he would marry the woman for whom the glass slipper had been made. The couriers began by trying the slipper on all the princesses. They tried it on the duchesses and then on the ladies of the court. But nowhere in the land could they find a woman whose foot was small enough to fit the slipper.

At last it was brought to the two sisters. They pushed and pushed, trying to squeeze their feet inside, but they were not able to manage it. Cinderella was in the room and recognized her slipper at once. "Let me see if it will fit my foot," she said.

Her sisters began to laugh and tease her. But the courier who was sent with the slipper looked at Cinderella and saw that she was lovely. He said his orders were that every woman in the land should try it on.

Cinderella sat down and he held the slipper up to her little foot. It went on at once, as easily as if it had been made of wax. Then, while the two sisters watched in astonishment, Cinderella drew from her pocket the other glass slipper and put it on too. Suddenly her godmother was there and she touched the girl's ragged clothes with her wand and they became a gown even more beautiful than the ones she had worn to the ball.

And now her two sisters knew she had been the unknown princess they had so admired. They threw themselves at her feet

to beg her forgiveness for all their ill treatment. Cinderella took them up and embraced them and said that she forgave them with all her heart.

Then Cinderella was taken before the prince. He was overwhelmed with love for her and some time later they were married. Cinderella, who was as good as she was beautiful, gave her two sisters a home in the palace, and that very same day they were married to two lords of the court.

HANSEL AND GRETEL

The Brothers Grimm

At the edge of a large forest there once lived a woodcutter with his wife and two children. The boy was called Hansel and the girl, Gretel. They were always very poor and had little to live on. But at last a terrible famine came to the land, and the woodcutter could not even provide food for his family.

One night he lay awake in bed, worrying over his troubles. "What is to become of us?" he said to his wife. "How can we feed our poor children when we have nothing for ourselves?"

"I'll tell you what," she answered. "Tomorrow morning we will take the children out to the thickest part of the forest. We will light a fire and give them each a piece of bread. Then we will go about our work and leave them there. They won't be able to find their way home, and so we shall be rid of them."

"No, I could never find it in my heart to leave my children alone in the forest," said the woodcutter. "The wild animals would soon come and tear them to pieces."

"What a fool you are!" the woman said. "Then we must all four die of hunger. You might just as well plane the boards for our coffins at once." And she gave him no peace until he consented.

But the two children had not been able to sleep for hunger, and so they heard what their stepmother had said.

Gretel wept bitterly. "All is over for us now."

"Be quiet, Gretel," said Hansel. "Don't cry. I'll find a way to save us."

When the woodcutter and his wife were asleep, Hansel got

up, put on his jacket, and slipped out the door. The moon was shining brightly, and the white pebbles around the house gleamed like silver coins. Hansel stooped down and gathered as many pebbles as his pockets would hold.

Then he went back to Gretel. "Go to sleep now," he said. "We will not perish in the forest." And he lay down and slept himself.

At daybreak, before the sun had risen, the woman came to wake them. "Get up, you lazybones," she ordered. "We are going into the forest to fetch wood." She gave them each a piece of bread. "Here is something for your dinner, but do not eat it right away, for it's all you'll get."

Gretel took the bread and put it under her apron because Hansel's pockets were filled with pebbles.

At length they all started out for the forest. When they had gone a little way, Hansel stopped to look back at the cottage, and he did it again and again.

"What are you doing?" his father asked. "Take care and keep up with us."

"Oh, Father," said Hansel, "I am looking at my white cat. It is sitting on the roof, saying good-bye to me."

"Little fool!" the woman said. "That is no cat. It's the morning sun shining on the chimney."

But Hansel had not been looking at the cat at all. Each time he stopped, he had dropped a white pebble on the ground to mark the way.

In the middle of the forest where the trees grew dense, their father made a fire to warm them. When it was blazing, the woman said, "Now lie down by the fire and rest while we go and cut wood. We will soon come back to fetch you."

Hansel and Gretel sat by the fire, and when dinnertime came, they each ate their little bit of bread. They thought their father was quite near because they could hear the sound of an axe. They did not realize it was not an axe at all, but a branch he had tied to a dead tree so that the wind blew it back and forth. The children sat so long that at last they fell fast asleep.

When they awoke, it was dark night. Gretel began to cry. "How shall we ever get out of the forest?"

But Hansel comforted her. "Wait until the moon rises," he said. "Then we will find our way."

When the full moon rose, Hansel took his sister by the hand, and they began to walk, guided by the pebbles that glittered like bits of silver.

They walked the whole night through, and at daybreak they finally reached their father's cottage.

"You bad children!" said the woman when she saw them. "Why did you sleep for so long in the forest? We thought you did not mean to come back here anymore."

But their father was glad, for it had hurt him sorely to leave them behind.

Not long afterward they were again in great need, and Hansel and Gretel heard the woman at night talking to the woodcutter. "We have only half a loaf left and when we have eaten that, we will have nothing. The children must go away. We will take them farther into the forest so that they will not find their way back. There is nothing else to be done."

The woodcutter tried to protest, but it was no use. Because he had given in to her the first time, he was forced to agree.

When everything was quiet, Hansel again got up, meaning to go after more pebbles, but the woman had locked the door and he couldn't get outside. Still he consoled his sister. "Don't cry, Gretel. Go to sleep. There is nothing to fear."

In the early morning the woman made the children get up, and she gave them each a bit of bread, but it was smaller than before. On the way to the forest Hansel crumbled his piece in his pocket and stopped again and again to drop the crumbs on the ground.

"Hansel, what are you stopping for?" asked his father.

"I am looking at my dove, who is sitting on the roof and wants to say good-bye to me."

"Little fool!" said the woman. "That is no dove. It's the morning sun shining on the chimney."

But Hansel continued to strew the crumbs behind him on the ground.

The woman led the children far into the forest to a place where they had never been before. Again they made a big fire.

"Stay where you are, children," she said. "And when you are tired, you may go to sleep. We are going farther on to cut wood, and in the evening we will come back and fetch you."

At dinnertime Gretel shared her bread with Hansel, for he had left his behind to mark the way. They went to sleep, and the evening passed, but no one came to fetch them.

It was dark when they woke up. Hansel comforted his sister and held her close. "Wait until the moon rises," he said. "Then we can see the bread crumbs that I scattered for a path."

When the moon rose, they started out but they found no bread crumbs. They did not know that all the thousands of birds who lived in the forest had swooped down and eaten every one.

"We shall soon find the way," said Hansel. But they could not find it. They walked all night and the next day, but they could not get out of the forest.

They were very hungry, for they had found only a few berries to eat. At last they could not go farther and so they lay down and went to sleep.

When they awoke in the morning, it was the third day since they had left their father's cottage. They started to walk again but they only went deeper into the forest, and they began to fear that if no help came they would perish.

Then at midday they saw a beautiful snow-white bird. It sang so sweetly that they stood still to listen. When the bird stopped singing, it fluttered its wings and flew near them. Hansel and Gretel followed it until they came out into a clearing, and there they saw a little house, wonderful beyond their dreams.

The house was made entirely of cake, and it was roofed with icing. The windows were transparent sugar. The children were so hungry that they did not hesitate at all. Hansel stretched up and broke off a piece of the roof, and Gretel went to the window and began to nibble at that. Then a gentle voice called out to them:

"Nibbling, nibbling like a mouse,
Who's that nibbling at my house?"

The children answered:

"Just the winds, the winds that blow
From the sky to the earth below."

All at once the door opened and an old, old woman hobbled out, holding tightly to a cane. Hansel and Gretel were so frightened that the food they were eating fell from their hands.

But the old woman only shook her head. "Ah, dear children," she said. "Come in and stay with me. You will come to no harm."

She took them by their hands and led them into the little house. A fine dinner was set before them, pancakes and sugar, milk, apples, and nuts. After they had eaten, she took them to two small white beds. Hansel and Gretel crept beneath the blankets, and when they fell asleep, they felt as if they were in heaven.

But the old woman who had seemed so kind was really a witch. She had built the cake house especially to lure the children to her.

Witches have red eyes and can't see very far, but their sense of smell is as keen as an animal's, and they know when human beings come close. The witch liked children best of all. Whenever she snared one, she cooked it and ate it and considered it a grand feast.

As soon as Hansel and Gretel were asleep she laughed wickedly. "Now I have them," she said. "They shan't escape me."

Early in the morning, before the children awoke, she went again to look at them in their beds. "They will be tasty morsels," she murmured, gazing at their rosy cheeks.

She seized Hansel with her bony hand and carried him off to a little stable, where she shut him up and barred the door. Though he shrieked at the top of his lungs, she took no notice of him.

Then she went to Gretel and shook her awake. "Get up, you lazybones. Fetch some water and cook something nice for your brother. He is in the stable and has to be fattened. When he is nice and fat, I will eat him."

Gretel began to cry bitterly, but it was no use. She had to obey the witch's orders. The best food was to be cooked now

for Hansel, but Gretel had only the shells of crayfish to eat.

Every morning the old witch hobbled to the stable and ordered Hansel to hold out his finger so she could feel how fat he was.

But Hansel held out only a knuckle. The witch's eyes were dim, and she thought the bony knuckle was Hansel's finger and wondered why he did not get any fatter.

When four weeks had passed, she became very impatient and would wait no longer. "Now then, Gretel," she said. "Hurry along and fetch the water. Fat or thin, tomorrow I will kill Hansel and eat him."

How Gretel grieved! As she carried the water the tears streamed down her cheeks. "Oh, if only the wild animals in the forest had devoured us," she cried. "At least we would have died together."

"Stop your weeping! It will do you no good," said the witch.

Early in the morning she made Gretel fill the kettle and kindle a fire. "We will bake first," she said. "I have heated the oven and kneaded the dough. Creep in and see if the fire is blazing high enough now." And she pushed Gretel toward the oven.

The witch meant to shut the door and roast her once she was inside. But Gretel saw what she had in mind. "I don't know how to get in," she said. "How am I to manage it?"

"Stupid goose!" said the witch, rushing up to the oven. "The opening is big enough. See, I can fit myself."

Quickly Gretel gave the witch a push that sent her headlong into the flames, and then she banged the door and bolted it tight.

The witch howled horribly, but Gretel ran away and left her there to perish. She ran to the stable as fast as she could and opened the door.

"Hansel! Hansel!" she cried. "We are saved. The old witch is dead!"

Hansel rushed out like a bird from a cage when the door was opened. They fell upon each other and kissed each other and danced around with joy.

There was nothing more to fear, and so they went into the witch's house. In every corner they found chests full of pearls and precious jewels. Hansel filled his pockets and Gretel filled her apron, and then they hurried away out of the clearing.

Before they had gone far, they came to a great body of water. "We can't get across it," said Hansel. "I see no path and no bridge."

"Look there," Gretel told him. "A duck is swimming, and it will help us over if we ask it." Then she sang:

> "Little duck that cries quack, quack,
> Hansel and Gretel are waiting here.
> Please carry us upon your back,
> For no path or bridge is near!"

The duck came right up to them, and then it carried Hansel and Gretel across the water, one by one.

As they walked through the forest on the other shore, the trees and hills became more and more familiar to them. At last they saw their father's house in the distance.

Hansel and Gretel rushed inside and threw their arms around their father's neck. The poor man had not had a single moment of peace or pleasure since he had deserted his children in the forest, and while they were gone, his wife had died.

Gretel shook her apron and scattered the pearls and jewels all over the floor. Hansel added handful after handful out of his pockets.

From that time all their troubles were ended, and they lived together in great happiness.

RUMPELSTILTSKIN

The Brothers Grimm

There was once a miller who was very poor, yet his daughter was more beautiful than any maiden in the land. One day it happened that the miller met the king. "I have a daughter who can spin straw into gold," the miller said, trying in this way to make himself seem important.

"Is that so?" said the king. "Such a skill interests me greatly. Bring your daughter to the castle tomorrow and then we shall see what we shall see."

When the girl was brought to him, the king led her to a little room filled with straw. He gave her a spinning wheel and a winder and said, "Now you must set to work quickly. If by dawn tomorrow this straw has not been spun into gold, you will have to die." Then without a backward glance he left the room.

The girl heard a key turn in the lock. She was entirely alone and terrified, for she had not the least idea how straw could be spun into gold. The hours passed and it grew darker and darker, and at last she threw herself upon the straw, weeping for her life. Suddenly the door sprang open. Before her stood a tiny man; he was not even as tall as her waist.

"Good evening, my girl. Why are you weeping?" he said.

The girl answered, "I was told to spin gold out of straw and I don't know how to do it."

"What will you give me if I spin it for you?"

"You shall have my necklace," she said.

At this the little man seated himself before the spinning wheel and began to work. The wheel whirred and sang all

through the night and one by one the spools piled near it were filled with gold.

When the king unlocked the door and saw the glittering gold, his mouth fell open in astonishment. Yet he was not satisfied. "You did well, my dear. Now let us see how much more gold you can spin for me tonight." He led her to another room filled with straw and this one was much larger than the first. "If you value your life, you will spin it all by morning," he said.

Once again the girl began to weep. She had no more idea how it was done than the first time. Suddenly the door opened

and the little man appeared. "What will you give me if I spin the straw into gold?" he demanded.

"The ring from my finger," she said without hesitation.

And so he began to work again at the spinning wheel, and by morning he was done. Not a piece of straw remained in the room, only spools and spools of gold.

The king was delighted at the sight of so much gold, but he was a very greedy man and so he wanted still more. He led the miller's daughter to a third room, far bigger than the first two and filled to the top with straw. "Tonight you must spin all

this into gold. If you succeed you shall be my queen." The king no longer cared that she was only a miller's daughter. All he could think about were the riches he would gain.

When the girl was alone the little man came again and said for the third time, "What will you give me if I spin the straw into gold for you?"

"I have nothing more I can give you," she cried in dismay.

"Promise me your first child if you should become queen," the little man said.

"Who knows if that will ever happen," thought the maiden and so she agreed. Without another word the little man set to work, and soon all the straw was spun into gold. When the king came in and saw it, he celebrated his marriage to the girl at once. Now the miller's daughter was queen of the land.

About a year later a beautiful child was born to her. She had forgotten all about the little man, but she had made her promise and the very next day he was there in her room. "Now give me the child," he said.

The queen was horrified and told the little man he could have all the wealth of the kingdom if he would let her keep the child. But he cared nothing for riches. "I would far rather have some living thing," he said and he reached out his arms for the baby.

At this the queen began to weep and moan as if her heart would break. The little man took pity upon her and said, "I will give you three days and three days only. If within this time you discover my name you may keep the child."

During the night the queen remembered all the names she had ever known and she sent a messenger into the countryside to discover what other names there were. When the little man appeared the next day, she began to call them out one by one. "Are you Caspar? Are you Melchior? Are you Balzer?"

But each time he only shook his head and said, "No, that is not my name."

On the second day the messenger told the queen the most strange and unusual names from the farthest parts of the kingdom. "Perhaps your name is Cowribs?" she said to the little man when he came. "Perhaps it is Spindleshanks? Perhaps it is Lacelegs?"

"No, that is not my name," he said again and again, and now only one day remained.

The next morning the messenger returned to the palace, riding hard. "I have found no more names," he told the queen. "But as I came to a high mountain at the end of the forest, I saw a tiny little house and in front of the house a fire was burning and around it a strange little man was hopping on one leg and singing:

> 'Today I bake, tomorrow I brew,
> The next the queen's child I will claim.
> Lucky it is that no one knows
> That Rumpelstiltskin is my name.' "

How glad the queen was when she heard the name! Soon afterward the little man came back and asked, "Now what names have you for me today?"

"Is your name Klaus?" she said.

"No."

"Is it Heinz?"

"No."

"Is it perhaps Rumpelstiltskin?"

"The devil told you that! The devil told you that!" screamed the little man. In his rage he stamped his foot so hard on the ground that he sank in up to his waist.

And then, as the queen watched in horror, he seized his other leg with both his hands and tore himself in two.

THE SNOW QUEEN

Hans Christian Andersen

Long, long ago, when trolls still lived upon the earth, there was one more evil than all the others. He was called the devil. He loved to mock human beings, and so he invented a mirror that made everything that was beautiful and good appear strange and horrid.

At first the trolls only played with the mirror, holding it to the world and laughing at the reflections. But one day they flew up into the sky with it, and the mirror spun out of their hands. Down, down, down it fell, shattering into a million pieces. Some were as tiny as grains of sand, and when the wind came, it blew the pieces everywhere.

If one of these ever entered a person's eye, nothing looked right again. But far worse was the fate of someone whose heart was pierced by a sliver of the mirror. The person would soon forget the pain. He would go on as before, never knowing that the heart inside him had frozen into ice.

At a time when the tiniest fragments of the devil's mirror were still swirling through the air, a boy and a girl lived very near each other in a big city. The boy's name was Kai, and the girl's name was Gerda. They were good friends and loved nothing better than to play in the window gardens that leaned from the gables of their houses. In the summer they could sit under the rose trees and walk easily from one house to the other.

In the winter, when the windows were tightly closed and covered with ice, Gerda would run down the stairs and through the snowy yard to Kai's house. The two children heated copper coins upon the stove and pressed them to the windows. A perfect small peephole was made in this way, and they could see across the wintry sky.

"The white bees are swarming," said the old grandmother.

"Do they have a queen too?" asked Kai.

The grandmother nodded. "She always stays in the center of the swarm. On snowy nights she flies through the streets of the town and looks in at the windows. Perhaps you have seen the ice patterns she leaves behind."

"Yes, I've seen them!" exclaimed Kai, and then he knew that what the grandmother said was true.

Late that night, as Kai was getting ready for bed, he went to the window and looked out through his peephole. It was snowing softly. As Kai watched, the snowflakes piled one on the other until they took the shape of a woman. She was made of glittering ice. Her eyes shone like two stars, yet neither rest nor peace was in them. She nodded and beckoned to Kai. He jumped back in terror, and in that moment a shadow passed the window as if a great bird had flown by.

It was the last storm of winter. Soon the thaws came and the earth grew green. Once again roses bloomed in the window gardens, and the children were able to sit outside.

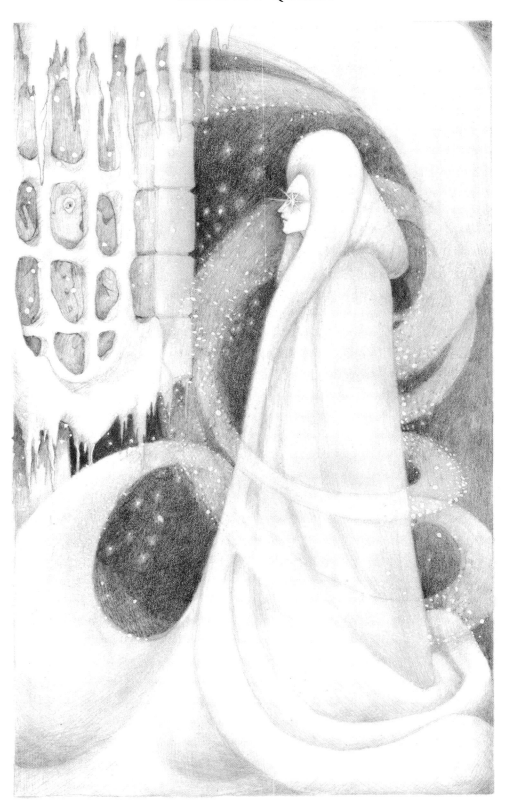

Late one afternoon, as the church bells struck the hour, Kai suddenly cried out.

"What is it?" asked Gerda.

"Something pricked my heart," Kai said, and then he gasped again. "Something sharp is in my eye."

Gerda looked into Kai's eyes. There was nothing to be seen, but she cried because she felt sorry for him.

"I think it is gone now," said Kai. But he was wrong. For one splinter of the devil's mirror had entered his eye, and the other had pierced his heart. Instantly he turned on Gerda and began to mock her. "Why are you crying? You look ugly when you cry. There is nothing the matter with me.

"Look!" he shouted. "That rose up there is growing all crooked, and that one has been eaten by a worm. How horrid they are!" Then he tore off the roses and stamped on them.

"What are you doing, Kai?" cried Gerda. And when he saw how frightened she was, he pulled off another flower and climbed through the window into his own house, leaving Gerda to sit outside all alone.

No longer would he consent to play with her. Now his games were more grownup. One winter day when snow was falling, he came by with his sled upon his back and wearing his woolen hat. He screamed into Gerda's ear as loudly as he could. "I have been allowed to go down to the square and play with the older boys!" And away he went without ever looking back.

Now it was the custom in that town for the bigger boys to tie their sleds to the farmers' carts. They would travel fast over the hard, packed snow and get a wonderful ride. While they were playing in this way, a big white sled came into the square and circled it twice. Quickly Kai tied his little sled to the big one. He wanted to show the older boys how daring he was.

Faster and faster they rode. Soon the town was far behind

them. Kai wanted to untie his sled, but each time he was about to do it, the driver smiled at him so kindly that he didn't. It was as if they were already friends. The snow fell more thickly. Snowflakes swirled around them, and the sled moved like the wind. Kai was very frightened. He tried to say his prayers, but he could remember only his multiplication tables.

The snowflakes grew and grew until they looked like white hens running near them. At last the big sled stopped and the driver stood up. Kai knew her at once. She was the Snow Queen!

"How cold you look," she said. "Come closer and let me warm you." She put her cloak around Kai and kissed his fore-head. Her kiss was like an icy wound, yet at once Kai felt stronger, and he did not notice how cold the air was. As he stared into the Snow Queen's face, he thought he had never seen anyone wiser or more beautiful. The longer he looked, the less he knew, and soon all memory of Gerda and the grandmother vanished.

They set out again, and now they left the earth and were flying in the air. They circled back over his town, but Kai did not even see it. Above oceans, lakes, and mountains they flew, spurred by the wind. He could hear the cry of the wolves and the cawing of the crows. The white moon came out and traveled with them across the sky. When daytime came, Kai slept at the feet of the Snow Queen.

It was a sad, gray winter. As time passed, people in the town began to say that Kai must have drowned in the icy river that ran close to the square where the boys played with their sleds. But Gerda could not believe this.

One clear morning in early spring she put on her new red shoes and crept out of the house. Down to the river she went and threw her shoes into the water. "Is it true that you have taken Kai?" she asked the river. "Here are my new red shoes if you will give him back to me."

The shoes struck the water far from shore, but the river carried them back to her as if to say it had not taken Kai. Gerda did not understand. She thought she had not thrown the shoes far enough, so she climbed into a rowboat that was in the reeds and threw the shoes over the water again. Just then the boat drifted with the current, and Gerda found herself floating down the river.

"Perhaps it will carry me to where Kai is," thought Gerda, and she sat perfectly still in her stocking feet. The land along the shores was green and beautiful, and sparrows flew near the boat, chirping as if to comfort her. At last the boat drifted near a

cherry orchard and came to rest upon the shore.

An old lady came out of a strange little house nearby and caught hold of the boat with her shepherd's crook. "You poor little thing," she said to Gerda. "Tell me who you are and how you have come to be here."

"I am searching for my playmate," said Gerda, and she told the old woman everything.

"You must not be sad. Your friend will probably pass this way soon. Come and eat my cherries and I will show you all the flowers in my garden." The old woman took Gerda by the hand and led her into the house. The windows were made of colored glass and a strange light shone in the room. On a table stood a silver bowl full of ripe cherries. As Gerda ate them and stayed with the woman, she thought of Kai less and less.

The old woman knew witchcraft, but she was not evil, and she had always wanted a little girl. That evening, when Gerda had fallen asleep, the woman went into the garden and pointed her shepherd's crook at the rose trees. At once they sank into the ground and disappeared. She was afraid that if Gerda saw the roses, she would think of Kai and run away.

In the morning she took the girl outside and showed her the garden. Gerda played in the golden sunshine with the flowers and came to know every one. But always something seemed to be missing, and she could not think what it was.

Many weeks passed and Gerda might have stayed forever, lulled by the old woman's kindness and the beauty of the place. But one day she noticed the painting of a rose on a broad-brimmed hat the woman often wore. At once she leaped up and ran outside. Why were there no roses among all the flowers in the garden? Gerda was so sad that she wept, and where her tears fell, a rose tree suddenly grew up. She breathed in the fragrance of the flowers and thought of the roses at home and of Kai.

"I have stayed here far too long!" she cried. "I must find Kai. Do you know where he is?" she asked the roses.

"He is not dead," they answered. "We have been down under the earth where the dead people are, and Kai was not there."

Gerda ran among the flowers, asking all of them if they had seen Kai. But though the flowers sang to her, they knew only the words to their own songs.

In despair Gerda ran from the garden and unlatched the door in the garden wall. Outside, the earth was cold and gray. Suddenly Gerda realized that it was late autumn. Back in the old woman's garden she had not seen the seasons change. There, it was always summer, and the flowers of every season bloomed at once.

"I have wasted so much time," thought Gerda. "I must not wait here any longer." She walked through fields and forests, though there was frost on the ground and her bare feet stung. The leaves on the trees had turned to yellow, and a cold autumn mist dripped down through their branches. How harsh and sad the world seemed!

Finally Gerda found herself in a dark forest. In the evening it began to snow. Then there was a whoosh of dark wings, and a large crow landed near her. "Caw, caw," he cried.

By this Gerda knew he was greeting her in a friendly way. "Do you know where my friend Kai is?" she asked him.

"Perhaps," said the crow slowly. "There is a castle not far from here and in it lives a princess. Recently she has taken a husband, a young man who is a stranger and is rumored to be afraid of nothing."

Gerda cried out in excitement. "That must be Kai!"

"Well, perhaps," the crow answered. "He is said to have long hair and bright, shining eyes. Many before him had tried to win the princess. But it was the stranger she wanted, because he was far cleverer than all the rest."

"Now I know it is Kai," said Gerda. "He is so clever that he can figure in fractions. Won't you take me to the castle, dear crow? I must see him at once."

The crow looked thoughtfully at Gerda, and then he nodded. "This way," he said. And he rose up into the air and flew ahead of her out of the forest.

As they entered the castle Gerda was nearly faint with longing. She was certain the bridegroom must be Kai. Soon she would see his face. He would smile at her and tell her how happy he was that she had found him at last.

Gerda followed the crow up the back stairs to the bridal chamber. The castle was dim and quiet. But suddenly there was a whirling, rushing sound, and shadows of horses and hunters, of dogs and falcons, moved upon the walls. Gerda drew back fearfully.

"Do not be afraid," said the crow. "They are only dreams come to fetch the princess and her bridegroom. They will be fast asleep, and you will learn if he is the one you seek."

At last they arrived in the royal bedchamber. Gerda peeked at the bridegroom where he lay and saw his long brown hair upon the pillow. "It is Kai!" she shouted with joy. Then the dreams rushed in again, and the young man awoke and looked her in the face.

But it was not Kai, not Kai at all!

With no thought for where she was, Gerda began to weep. "You poor thing," said the prince. "Tell us what is the matter."

As Gerda told them all that had happened, the princess held

her close. They said she must spend the night, and in the morning when she awoke, they gave her a silk dress and a pair of boots and a golden coach drawn by four horses. For a time the crow rode with her. But when they came to the edge of the forest, he had to fly away. Gerda waved and waved until she could no longer see his wings shining in the distance. Now she was alone and felt sadder and more desolate than ever.

At length they came to a stand of trees along the roadside. Hidden among them was a band of robbers and the golden coach dazzled their eyes like a flame. "Gold! Gold!" they screamed, flinging themselves upon it. They grabbed hold of the horses and killed the coachman, and then they dragged Gerda out upon the road.

"She is lovely and plump," said an old robber woman. "I think I will have her for supper." She took a long knife from her belt, and her eyes sparkled with greed.

But just as the robber woman was about to slit poor Gerda's throat, her daughter, whom she was carrying upon her back, bit her hard. "No, she is mine. I want to play with her," said the little robber girl. She was a spoiled and willful child, and so the robbers had to give in.

Late that night, when they arrived at the robbers' castle, the girl asked Gerda if she was a princess.

"No, I am not," answered Gerda, and then she told her how she was looking for Kai and had come to be riding in such a fine carriage.

The robber girl looked very seriously at her then and nodded. "I won't allow them to kill you even if I do get angry at you. I will do it myself."

Gerda was very frightened. The walls of the robbers' castle were black with smoke, and ravens flew in and out of the tower. Dogs roamed freely through the halls. They jumped up in the air but they did not bark; that was not permitted.

In the corner where the robber girl slept were all her pet animals. Two wood pigeons were kept in a cage high up in the rafters, and a reindeer stood tied near her bed. "I like to keep them imprisoned," she told Gerda. "It amuses me to see their sorrow."

The little robber girl went to sleep with her knife clutched in her hand, but Gerda was afraid to close her eyes. She did not know if she was going to live or die. In the middle of the night, suddenly one of the wood pigeons cooed. "We have seen Kai. He sat in the Snow Queen's sled and white hens ran near them. She has carried him to a land far to the north. You must ask the reindeer where it is. He will know."

"Oh, yes. Ice and snow are always there. It is a wonderful place," the reindeer said. "There an animal can roam freely in the shining valleys. That is where I was born." Then he grew silent, remembering all he had lost.

In the morning Gerda told the robber girl what she had heard from the animals. The girl listened quite solemnly and then jumped out of bed and hugged Gerda. "I will help you. Leave me your pretty dress and your boots. You shall take the reindeer. He will carry you to your friend."

She tied Gerda onto the reindeer's back and gave her some meat and two loaves of bread. Away they went, as fast as they could, farther and farther north. They heard the wolves howl and the ravens call, and suddenly the sky was filled with great arcs of color. They were the northern lights.

At last they came to a little cottage at the border of Lapland. An old woman came out, and they told her where they were bound. "You must find my friend, the Finnish woman. She will be able to help you," the old woman said. She wrote a note on a piece of dried codfish, and they set out once more.

When they reached the Finnish woman's house, they had to knock on the chimney, for the door was nearly buried under the snow. But inside the house it was as hot as an oven. The Finnish woman gave the reindeer a piece of ice to cool his head and read three times what was written on the codfish.

Poor Gerda was so tired that she fell asleep in the corner.

Then the reindeer and the Finnish woman talked together quietly. "You are very wise," the reindeer said. "Can't you make a magic drink so that Gerda will be able to defeat the Snow Queen?"

The woman smiled at him and patted his nose. "I can give her no more power than she has already. Don't you see how people and animals must serve her? Don't you see how she has been able to journey so far, though her feet are bare? No, my friend, Gerda's power is in her heart. Her goodness and innocence are the only weapons against the Snow Queen." She woke Gerda up then and lifted her onto the reindeer's back.

He ran a short way over the snowy earth and set her down beside a bush with red berries. It was at the edge of the Snow Queen's gardens. Gerda looked back at him only once and saw that his face was streaked with tears. Then she followed the path and ran toward the Snow Queen's palace as fast as she could.

Suddenly she saw hundreds of snowflakes. They whirled along just above the earth, growing larger as they came near. Some looked like huge porcupines, others like snakes writhing together; still others were like bears with cruel, grinning faces. All the snowflakes were blindingly white and horribly alive. They were the Snow Queen's army on the march.

Gerda stopped short. Her breath came fast, forming vapor in the frozen air. As she stood there it became more solid and shaped itself into a band of angels armed with shields and spears. They threw their spears at the snow creatures, shattering them into thousands of pieces. There were no more barriers after that, and Gerda was able to walk into the Snow Queen's palace.

The palace walls were glittering ice, and the windows and doors were made of wind. In the glare of the northern lights Gerda could see the gates opening before her. Echoing, vast, and cold was the Snow Queen's palace. Yet Gerda had come so far already and she was not afraid.

She ran through halls of drifted snow that turned and twisted for miles. At last she saw a tiny figure, blue with cold, seated on a frozen lake. As Gerda drew closer she saw that it was Kai. He was playing with pieces of ice, arranging them into patterns. The game was very important because the Snow Queen had promised that if he could form the right word she would give him the world and a new pair of skates. The word was "eternity," but Kai could not remember it no matter how hard he tried.

He did not even look up when Gerda rushed at him and threw her arms around his poor, stiff body. She began to cry, and her hot tears fell upon his heart and melted the ice away. Only then could he see her.

"Gerda, oh, Gerda. Is it really you? Where have you been for so long? What place is this, Gerda? Why is it so cold and empty here?" As he looked around him Kai burst into tears. He wept and wept until the grain of glass in his eye was washed away. Then he held on to Gerda as if he would never let her go.

So glad were they to be together that they never even noticed that the pieces of ice had formed themselves into the word Kai had been trying to make. Now the Snow Queen could return, and it would not matter, for Kai's right to freedom was written upon the frozen lake.

Then Gerda took his hand and they walked out of the Snow Queen's palace. They spoke of the grandmother and of the roses that bloomed in the window gardens. The wind had died down and the sun shone through the clouds. At last they reached the bush where the reindeer was waiting. Now there was a younger one, too, whose udder was full of warm milk for them to drink. Kai and Gerda climbed upon the reindeers' backs and the animals carried them along until blades of grass started to break through the snow.

"Good-bye, good-bye," the children called to the reindeer when they had come to a place where it was early spring. Here they heard birds singing and saw that the trees were all in bud. The towers of their own city were shining in the distance.

Soon they were walking up the stairs to the grandmother's house. Nothing had changed. The clock on the wall was ticking and the wheels inside it moved. But when Kai and Gerda stepped through the doorway, they knew that they had grown up. They were no longer children.

In the window gardens they saw the roses blooming. There were the little stools they used to sit upon. As they went out into the sunshine all memory of the Snow Queen's palace and its empty splendor vanished. There they sat, the two of them, and it was summer, a beautiful summer day.

THUMBELINA

Hans Christian Andersen

Once there was a woman who wanted a child more than anything in the world. At last in loneliness and sorrow she went to a witch and spoke of her desire.

"That's as easy as winking!" said the witch. "Take this seed and plant it in a flowerpot filled with good, rich earth. Water it carefully and guard it very well."

The woman did as the witch had said. The first time she watered the seed, a large and brilliant flower sprang up. It was still in bud, its petals tightly closed.

The woman bent to kiss the flower. But the moment her lips touched the silky petals, they began to open. The woman could not believe her eyes. There inside sat a tiny little girl. She was perfectly formed, as graceful as the flower from which she'd come. When the woman held her, she discovered that she was not even the size of her thumb.

Though she was a wonderful child in every way, she never grew at all. She was called Thumbelina and was treated with great extravagance and care. Her cradle was a polished walnut shell; each night she slept between fresh flower petals. In the daytime she liked to sit on a table and sing in the sunlight. Her voice was very beautiful—high and haunting and silvery.

One night as she lay sleeping, a toad hopped in at the window. "What a lovely wife for my son!" she said. Without even looking around her, she took up the walnut shell and hopped off with it to her home by the edge of a stream.

"Here, look what I brought you," said the toad proudly to

her son. But the only sound he could utter was *"Koax, koax, brekke-ke-kex."*

"Don't talk so loud or you will wake her," complained the toad. "She might still run away from us, for she is light as swan's down."

Holding the walnut shell high, the toad swam out into the stream to an eddy where masses of water lilies grew. On a leaf far from shore she put the cradle. Then she went back to build a new room in the mud for the bride.

In the morning Thumbelina woke up and looked all around her at the great arching sky. She felt her cradle rock with the motion of the stream and cried out in terror.

The fish swimming in the water below came to the surface and looked curiously at Thumbelina. "Oh, please help me," she said. "I must get away from here."

And so the fish began to gnaw at the lily stalk with their sharp little teeth.

At last the leaf broke free and floated down the stream. Away went Thumbelina, gently spinning with the current. Gradually her fear left her, and she began to enjoy the journey. Never before had she been outside.

A beautiful butterfly flew near her. Fascinated by its gossamer wings, Thumbelina sat very still to show she meant no harm. The butterfly kept darting toward the sash on her dress, and Thumbelina thought to fasten one end loosely around it. She held on to the other end, and the butterfly flew along, pulling the lily pad behind like a little toy boat.

Thumbelina glided much faster now, but as night came on, she saw that the butterfly was growing weary. She called it to her and asked that it take her to shore. Gently she unfastened the sash. The butterfly hovered near her for a time, then slowly flew off. Thumbelina felt sad as she watched it disappear. Now she was truly alone, and the place was a foreign land to her.

The whole summer through Thumbelina lived by herself at the edge of the stream. She wove a bed of grass stems and hung it like a hammock under a large, spreading leaf to shelter herself from the rain. She sipped nectar from the flowers and drank the dew that lay on the leaves at dawn.

But when summer ended, the plants and flowers withered. The birds that had sung to her flew away, and there was frost on the ground each morning. Thumbelina's clothes were in rags, and she shivered with the cold. Autumn passed, and then one day it began to snow. Each snowflake fell like a veil upon her. She feared that she would be buried or that she would freeze to death. "Run!" she thought. She must run to find shelter.

The snow came at her in white swirling clouds, and she stumbled along until she came to a large cornfield. Suddenly she saw a hole that tunneled down into the earth. It would be warmer there perhaps and the snow would not reach her. But when Thumbelina ran toward the hole, a field mouse appeared before her. "Come," said the creature and beckoned her to follow.

As they descended into the tunnel, Thumbelina realized that she was in the snug, small home of the field mouse. Corn was piled up all around her, and its smell was in the air.

"Please," said Thumbelina, "could I have a bit of corn to eat?"

"You poor, dear thing!" the field mouse answered kindly. "You had better come into my room and have dinner with me."

The two got on well together, and after some days the field

mouse invited Thumbelina to work for her and stay the winter. Late one evening she said to dust the floor and polish everything in the room until it shone. An important visitor was coming to call.

This was a mole who was very rich and wore a sleek velvet coat. But he was blind. He hated the sun and mocked all the creatures who lived outdoors. The field mouse, however, was impressed by the mole's riches. She told Thumbelina to sing for him and tell stories of her travels. As he listened to Thumbelina's beautiful voice, the mole fell in love with her.

The next time he came to visit, he said he would show them his rooms underground. By the pale light of a piece of torchwood, he led them through a long, twisting passage. Suddenly they came upon a swallow lying sprawled and dead in the passageway. Thumbelina felt sorry for the swallow, but the mole kicked at him with his stumpy legs. "What a pitiful life to be a bird," he said. "A creature who does nothing all day but fly from branch to branch deserves to starve to death in winter."

Thumbelina said nothing, but at night she crept out of bed and wove a blanket of hay. Taking up some torchwood for a lantern, she carried the blanket to the dead bird so that he might lie comfortably on the cold ground.

"Good-bye, swallow," she said. "It might have been you who sang to me this summer when all the trees were green." She laid her head on his soft feathers for a moment, then darted back in fright. Something moved inside him with the slow, steady rhythm of a heartbeat. The bird was not dead; he was merely numbed with cold. The warmth of the blanket and of Thumbelina's body had stirred him back to life.

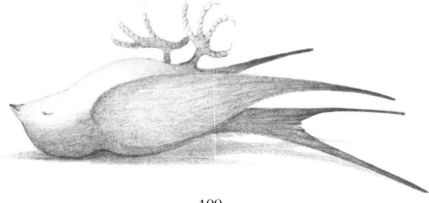

Each night after that she crept out of bed to tend the swallow. As he grew stronger, he told her how he had torn his wing on a thornbush. The other swallows had flown away to the warm countries, but he had not been able to keep up with them. At last he could go no farther and had plummeted to the ground.

Thumbelina cautioned him never to move from where he lay, for if the field mouse and the mole knew he was alive, they would surely kill him.

When spring warmed the earth once more, Thumbelina knew it was time for the swallow to go. His wing had healed now. Each night he fluttered it over and over again, strengthening it for flying. "Won't you come with me?" he asked her. "You can easily sit upon my back, and I will carry you away into the leafy woods."

But Thumbelina could not bring herself to abandon the field mouse who had kept her from starving. She made a hole in the roof of the passageway and watched longingly as the swallow flew out into the sunshine. She felt that all the pleasure in her life was going with him.

Every evening now the mole came to call on Thumbelina. He made her sing until her voice grew hoarse. Whenever she stopped, he prodded her to continue. This was the way he loved her. Without ever once asking Thumbelina, the mole and the field mouse agreed that she would be married to him in the autumn.

Suddenly there was a hum of activity in the field mouse's room, for she had insisted that the bride have a wardrobe of new clothes. Four spiders were hired to weave day and night, and Thumbelina was put to work spinning linen thread from flax. The mole felt it was all for him. He liked to sit in his chair and listen to the whirring sound of the spinning wheel.

But Thumbelina wept bitterly. Every morning when the

sun rose and every evening when it set, she was allowed to go to the doorsill and stand outside. In the heat of August the corn had grown as high as a forest. When the wind blew the stalks apart, she could see bright pieces of sky. How beautiful it was! She did not know how she would live deep inside the earth with the mole, whom she now despised more than ever.

As the time of her wedding drew closer, she sobbed out her fears to the field mouse. "Nonsense," the field mouse said. "Don't be stubborn or I'll bite you with my white teeth. His velvet coat is handsome, and the food in his pantry is fit for a queen."

Thumbelina understood then that she was trapped as surely

as if she were in a cage. Summer was ending, and she knew she would never be able to survive outside through the harsh, cold months of winter.

But now the wedding day had come. For the last time she crept to the doorsill to stand in the sunshine. She knew the mole would never permit her to leave his side. She wept as she felt the warmth upon her face and made ready to go back into the earth. Then suddenly above her she heard a shower of notes, a glorious morning song.

She looked up, and there was the swallow.

"The cold winter is coming again," he said, flying down to her. "I've looked for you many times, and now I must fly away to the warm countries. Won't you come with me? I'll take you to where it is always summer."

This time Thumbelina did not hesitate. She climbed upon the swallow's back and tied her sash to one of his feathers. Then he rose up into the sky.

They flew over forests and fields, high above mountains with snow-capped peaks. When Thumbelina felt cold in the bleak air, she crept in under his feathers. It was so secure and close, a coverlet of softest down.

At last they arrived in the warm countries. The sun beat down upon the earth and the light was clear as crystal. Lemons and oranges hung on the trees and sweet spices perfumed the air.

The swallow flew on until they came to a dazzling white palace. In the pillars were many nests, and one of these was the swallow's home.

"I dearly love you and yearn to keep you with me," said the swallow sadly. "But I do not think you could live up high as I do, for when the wind comes, you might fall. Why don't you take one of the flowers that grows below for your home. At least we shall be neighbors."

Thumbelina did not remember that she had lived before in a flower, but the idea seemed to her a good one. The swallow set her gently on the petals of a brilliantly colored flower; then she slid inside.

But this could not be, she thought. The home was already taken!

A young man was standing there, shining as if he had been made of glass. A silver crown was on his head and gauzy wings grew from his back.

"Isn't he wonderful?" Thumbelina whispered to the swallow, who still hovered nearby. Never before had she seen a person just her size.

When the young man got over his fright at the closeness of the great bird, he explained to Thumbelina that a small person lived in each of the flowers; he was their king. Then he took off his crown and placed it upon Thumbelina's head. "You are so lovely," he said. "Won't you be my queen?"

Thumbelina never thought to refuse. She could tell he was kind by the sound of his voice and the curve of his mouth. She felt that at last she had come home.

Then the king declared that there was to be a welcoming party more joyful than any seen before in the land. From all the flowers men and women came, bringing gifts for Thumbelina. But the most wonderful was a pair of tiny wings that could be fastened to her back so she too could dart among the flowers. Everyone danced all night, and above them in his nest was the swallow, singing for them his most heartbreaking tune.

LIST OF SOURCES

Andersen, Hans Christian. *Andersen's Fairy Tales,* trans. Mrs. E. V. Lucas and Mrs. H. B. Paull. New York: Grosset, 1945.

Andersen, Hans Christian. *Danish Fairy Legends and Tales,* trans. Caroline Peachey. London: George Bell & Sons, 1907.

Andersen, Hans Christian. *Fairy Tales,* trans. R. P. Keigwin. New York: Scribner, 1950.

Andersen, Hans Christian. *Hans Andersen's Fairy Tales,* trans. Reginald Spink. New York: Dutton, 1958.

Andersen, Hans Christian. *It's Perfectly True: And Other Stories,* trans. Paul Leyssac. New York: Harcourt, Brace & World, 1938.

The Complete Grimm's Fairy Tales. New York: Pantheon Books, 1944.

Grimm, Brothers. *German Popular Stories and Fairy Tales,* trans. Edgar Taylor. London: George Bell and Sons, 1908.

Grimm, Brothers. *Grimms' Fairy Tales,* trans. Mrs. E. V. Lucas, Lucy Crane, and Marian Edwardes. New York: Grosset & Dunlap, 1945.

Grimm, Brothers. *Grimms' Tales for Young & Old: The Complete Stories,* trans. Ralph Manheim. Garden City: Doubleday & Co., Inc., 1977.

Grimm, Brothers. *Grimms' Household Tales,* trans. Marian Edwardes. New York: Dutton, 1922.

Grimm, Brothers. *Household Stories from the Collection of the Brothers Grimm,* trans. Lucy Crane. London: Macmillan, 1922.

LIST OF SOURCES

Haviland, Virginia, comp. *The Fairy Tale Treasury*. New York: Coward, McCann & Geoghegan, Inc., 1972.

Jacobs, Joseph. *English Fairy Tales,* 3rd ed. rev. New York: G. P. Putnam's Sons.

LePrince de Beaumont, Marie. *Beauty and the Beast,* trans. P. H. Muir. New York: Limited Editions, 1949.

Perrault, Charles. *The Fairy Tales of Charles Perrault,* trans. Norman Denny. London: Bodley Head, 1950.

Perrault, Charles, Mme. d'Aulnoy, and Mme. LePrince de Beaumont. *Favourite French Fairy Tales,* retold by Barbara Douglas. New York: Dodd, Mead & Co., 1921.

Perrault, Charles. *Old-Time Stories told by Charles Perrault,* trans. A. E. Johnson and others. New York: Dodd, Mead & Co., 1961.

Perrault, Charles. *The Tales of Mother Goose,* trans. Charles Walsh. Boston: Heath, 1901.

ABOUT THE ADAPTER AND ILLUSTRATOR

AMY EHRLICH has written more than fifteen books for children. She has done three retellings of individual fairy tales, but *The Random House Book of Fairy Tales* is her first collection. In preparing the text she read more than one hundred fairy tales and at least three different versions of each tale that she finally selected. "I tried to balance the tales for tone as well as subject matter—the earthy with the lyrical, the rogues with the princesses. But in the process of selection I learned that the tales that have come down to us from childhood, those we want to pass on to our own children, have endured because they are, quite simply, the best."

DIANE GOODE has illustrated many highly praised children's books, including the 1983 Caldecott Honor Book, *When I Was Young in the Mountains.*

About her work on *The Random House Book of Fairy Tales,* Ms. Goode says, "This work was done to size on opaline parchment, which is a smooth, almost translucent surface. I sketched lightly in pencil and then, using colored pencils, blocked out all the large areas. Then I came back with a tiny sable brush and watercolors to bring out the details. I never use black for outlines—I prefer either dark brown or a color. But I expect my materials to keep changing, just as my approach to each book changes—it's all fluid. I don't have any particular routine as I work, and I try not to plan too far ahead; I prefer the work to evolve out of itself. I visualize illustrations while I read the manuscript, then sit down and see how it goes. As I work I think about the story, the scenes, the characters, the mood and the style, the costumes and the locale, and I make choices—creating, shaping, and coloring the special, individual world of each tale.

"I feel that the whole process of illustrating is a privilege and a pleasure, almost as if my childhood fantasies have come true."